Complicated

Mental

Pain

Complicated Mental Pain

BY ROSHINAIE JOHNSON

Chapter 1

Alright. Let's just cut straight to it. I'm getting this out of the way because I don't want any more shocked stares, rude gasps, or questions. I'm sick of that stuff. I know I'm going to have to deal with it more in life because it is human nature, and I guess I can understand why people are so stunned, but I can at least eliminate them doing the prior things I mentioned.

So look. Yes I was fourteen when I got pregnant with my first child. I was young, fast and had a lot of freedom. My mom never paid attention to me. She didn't raise me. It's like she didn't care about me. She was always out living the good life, and I was always at home alone. At least that's what she thought until I wound up pregnant with my first.

Look. Don't call me stupid. Some people don't even think a fourteen year old can get pregnant even thought I'm sitting here saying I did. I'm not lying. Why would I? Saying I have no kids would eliminate at least some of those stares and gasps. I was fourteen when I got pregnant with my Josiah. Then I had Justin, and then Alisa. Whoever can't believe that better hold on tight because I have my Lanice and Charise too. Yes, that's right.

And they all have the same daddy.

My mom was so mad I had all those kids. Her and everyone else in the world couldn't believe it. I was the talk of everybody's conversation at school and all of my mother's friend's conversations.

It was rough raising my kids. Not because they were bad, but because five people taking turns screaming and hollering for one thing or another is enough to drive anyone up a wall. Well, me at least.

My babies' daddy helped out a lot with my first four by stopping by to babysit, bringing them food, changing their diapers and bringing me money. He was a good father and we got along well. Everything was good until his parents decided to

1

move to Chicago when I was five months pregnant with what was their son's last child with me. I should've saw that coming after they tried to convince my mom to make me get an abortion. I definitely declined killing any of my kids because I knew as the days and years went on I would say to myself, *my kids would've been born today* or *my kids would've been five today.* Or whatever age that comes to mind first. I wouldn't be able to live knowing I denied them a chance at life. I can definitely understand my babies' daddy's parents being worried I would get pregnant again though.

My kids' dad's parents also probably wanted to move somewhere that the people didn't know their twenty-two year old son at the time had five kids. Today he doesn't call or visit my kids but I don't care and neither do they. They never bring him up. Not once have they asked me about their dad. I'm all they need. They love me unconditionally. They're father sends a nice check in the mail and we enjoy spending his money on outings and parties.

I have one more thing to say. When I was twenty I got pregnant again. And at twenty-one I got pregnant again. Bianca and Stacey are their names and they have a different dad from my other kids. Bianca and Stacey's dad was just for fun. I really wish I would've strapped up because I knew he would'nt be present in my kid's lives because he wasn't present in his other two kid's lives by another woman. I knew he was a hoe. I really should've used protection, but I'm glad I didn't. I love my little munchkins.

So there it is. I have seven kids.

And let me be the first to say that they are all good looking kids. Beyond handsome and beautiful. My first three are what the common black folks would refer to as red bones. My boys are so handsome, they are both taller than me. They have perfect shaped faces and nice builds. All the girls love my boys. My girls didn't get the height their dad's had. Thank goodness because I

2

didn't want a tall girl. They're absolutely flawless. They have cute shapes and gorgeous faces.

Chapter 2

I might as well say right here and now that even though I'm twenty-six now, I don't look twenty-six. I look like a teenager. I could pass for eighteen. People can't believe it when my kids call me mom.

My girls Charise and Lanice are what the common black folks would call yellow bones. They're just as stunning as their older sister. All I can do is hope my girls don't turn out like me and have a bunch of kids when they become teenagers. I haven't talked to them about sex yet but I plan to get around to it.

My youngest two are the same complexion as me. Brown. They're so fun. They always have me and their siblings dying laughing with their little impersonations.

"Mom can we order pizza?" my oldest son Josiah just rushed down the stairs and asked. He's eleven.

"I already did. It's on the way," I say. He kisses my cheek. I love my lil' big handsome man.

"Mama are we still going to shoot around tomorrow?" Josiah asks.

I can't even bring myself to say yes I'm so in aww of this boy. He's just too cute. I smile at him as he looks in my eyes. Even though he's been calling me mom for years. I love to hear him say it every time. He knows the answer is yes. He kisses my forehead and goes bac upstairs.

My kids are so perfect. They're looks alone could get them all types of gigs in the entertainment world. There's so many of us we could start our own reality show and put on our own fashion show.

Now I know, at first, I sounded rude, and probably a little harsh, but that's just because I'm so sick of judgmental people. I know what they are thinking when I get those annoying looks. They could at least try and keep their face at rest. I know people are not stupid. They know those stupid facials play over and over

again in people's minds. I have seven kids. Move on.

Now that that's out the way, I want to say that how I just said what I just said is only my attitude when I have to tell people the run down about my family. I hate it because no one needs to know, yet everyone is so nosy. I said it because I don't want anyone not paying attention to what I'm saying because they're trying to figure out how old I am and when I had my kids. I love my kids. I know I shouldn't have been having sex that young, but I don't regret any of them. They are my world.

And no. I'm not bitter. I'm Leah, I'm twenty-six years old and I have seven kids.

Let me say a little more about myself. I'm a writer. I write books for a living. I could write my life one day but I'm not. I just don't want to. My books are all selling really well. I wrote them when I was living with my mother at seventeen years old. I knew I needed to do something that wouldn't require me to leave the house because I needed to be with my kids, and at the same time would make me a lot of money. I knew I wanted to move out at eighteen years old so I worked my ass off writing day and night praying I could get out and make it on my own.

I didn't want to live with my mother anymore. She was never home and I hated catching her gossip with her friends about my kids.

My first book <u>Vicious Villains</u> became a best seller after only being on the shelf a month. It was about two brothers that tortured their abusive father for years when they found out he killed their mother and buried her in the backyard.

My second book <u>Time Pull</u> became a best seller. It was about a man who traveled to the future to come back and warn the world of what was going to happen to it. No one believed him when he said all animals would turn into carnivores and all the skyscrapers were going to collapse. The angry man spent years putting together a shelter for him family. He knew the exact date everything would happen but didn't tell anyone because no one

believed him. Not even his family, but he cared about them so he brought them to his shelter.

Both <u>Vicious Vilains</u> and <u>Time Pull</u> were done before I was eighteen. I racke dup all types of dough and got out of my mom's house. We lived in Minnesota at the time. At eighteen years old I drove me and my kids to California. We still stay in the same two story house in Hollywood. I have four bedrooms. My boys share a room. My three oldest girls share a room and my youngest two girls share a room. We love our lives.

Welcome to my house.

Chapter 3

Ding Dong. It's the doorbell. The pizza is here. Me and the kids get comfortable in our pajamas and eat in the living room watching a dance show Alisa likes to watch.

Me and my good looking children are spread out all over the living room floor and couches chowing down on food.

"Somebody used my bathing towel last night," my son Justin says looking at Bianca and Stacey.

"It wasn't me," Stacey says.

"It wasn't me either," Bianca says. "I don't even use no towel."

"Then what do you use?" I rush out. All the kids laugh.

"Just the soap," Bianca says. This girl is a trip. I love my little munchkin.

"Momma, can we go with you tomorrow to the school to work out?" Alisa asks.

"It's our turn to go," Justin says referring to himself and Josiah.

I have a seven seat car so I can never take all the kids with me anywhere.

When I need a sitter, my best friend Mya comes by. I never leave my kids home alone in fear that something might happen.

There may be a day when a cop pays my house a visit for some odd reason and asks to speak to an adult, then my kids might get taken away. A delivery boy might need an adult to sign for something. There's so many ways my family could get into a bad situation if I take a chance on leaving them by themselves.

Chapter 4

"Mya, they already ate breakfast so you can go back to sleep if you want," I say when she arrives the next morning.

Me and Mya have been cool for years. We met at a birthday party for one of Alisa's friends. Everyone knows how it is: the kids play while the parents sit and talk. Mya doesn't have any kids but she has a lot of cousins and brought one to the party.

Me and Mya got on the subject of careers. When she found out I was a writer, she asked me to write her story. She didn't have the type of cash I require to do the job so she's still paying it off today.

Usually, well actually I would never complete a task without being paid off, but Mya's story drew me in. I never met someone that was given away at birth, moved from foster home to foster home, beat at each one, ran away at sixteen and was never reported missing, and still managed to keep her right mind and tell the world how strong she is.

Mya was forced to stand in a room full of chemicals, punched in the face until she bled, yanked around by her hair, beat up, had bricks thrown at her back, was stabbed in the leg, and was hit by a car by her foster parents biological kids for fun.

I commend Mya for wanting the world to hear her story and at the same time, not using the real names of the people who mistreated her because she had faith that one day they would be better and feel remorseful for what they did to her. When that day comes, Mya didn't want to be the person to have given the world a constant reminder of who the abusers used to be.

Mya is really cool too, which is why I helped her out also. We became close while I wrote her story and my kids loved having her around. She couldn't believe I had five kids already when she met me. She said she admired the fact that I'm so young and raising all of them on my own. Especially when there's women with just three or less kids that still live with their

parents.

Mya works part-time at a phone store in the mall and watches my kids from time to time.

"Aye where's the remote?" Mya asks before I shut the front door. I feel in between the couches and find it. I toss it to her. "Thanks," she says.

"Alright. See you later," I say.

The boys jog with me around the track at a high school. I sprint a few times, jog a little and walk the curbs. I want to stay fit. Even though I have all these kids, I still have a nice athletic body. I have a slim waist and nice shape. I look just as good as my kids and I want to keep it that way. I'm not that much older than my kids. There's no excuse for me to be overweight.

Me and the boys stop by the gym before heading home. I like to see if anything's going on that I would enjoy watching. There's nothing. Just a bunch of boys shooting around and some men standing around and talking.

A ball rolls towards Josiah. He picks it up and shoots a corner shot behind the three-point line. He swishes it. A little boy, who looks like he's about three years old, chases after the ball and runs to bring it back to Josiah before we make it out the gym.

"Aye, shoot it again," one of the men talking says.

Josiah makes the same shot from the same spot. The little boy brings the ball back to Josiah again. Josiah makes it.

"You as good as your brother?" the same man asks looking at Justin. Justin makes a few shots and he's amazed. "I have a few returning players coming up here in a few minutes. You guys want to go up and down with thema few times?"

Justin and Josiah look at me for approval. I nod my head. They play one on one and shoot around until the players show up.

I'm shocked when I see the players. They're big as hell. I forgot we're at a high school and not the boy's middle school. I'm just not sure how this is going to turn out. I hope my boys

don't get too embarrassed. I've never really paid attention to t hem play basketball. When I take them to the park I'm either writing or talking on the phone while they do them.

The man that asked them to play hands them white jerseys.

The players stretch circled around one player.

I got my phone on record.

Jump ball goes up and is hit towards Justin who grabs it and scores a layup. He has the first points of the game. The other team takes the ball out and throws it down the court so they can return the favor, but Josiah's fast legs sprint down the court and steals it before it gets to the other player.

Josiah does all these moves: behind the back, between the legs and crossover before he tossed the ball up in the air for his post player that dunks it in. The other team doesn't have any points because my boys are so quick on their feet and quick with their hands.

This is unbelievable. I send Mya a clip of my boys playing and have her show the girls at home. My boys are showing out. They're playing like professionals.

Another man hands Josiah a black jersey. Now he's guarding Justin. This was a smart move. The game has slowed down tremendously. My boys defend and keep up with each other really well.

The boys scrimmage for thirty minutes and the same man that asked Josiah to shoot lets both my boys shoot around again. He's approaching me. "How old are they?"

"Josiah is fourteen," I lie. He can't believe his ears. "Well he will be in a few days. Are you the coach?"

"Yes. Coach Eric." He shakes my hand. "It's hard to believe I've never heard about these boys. How long have you guys been out here?"

"Maybe eight years," I say.

"Eight years and I've never heard a word about them?" Coach Eric says. He's shocked that word hasn't gotten around about my

handsome sons.

"Well they don't play on a team. They just play for fun," I say.

"Do they want to play on a team?" Coach Eric asks.

"It's something I never asked them," I say hiding my attitude the best way I can. "I figured they would express interest to me if they wanted to play like they do everything else."

"What about if I ask them?" Coach Eric asks.

"Go ahead," I say.

"What's their names?" Coach Eric asks.

"Justin and Josiah," I say. I call them over and Coach Eric pops the question. The boys shrug their shoulders like it's whatever. They don't care.

"Mom is it alright?" Justin asks.

"Yes. Go finish shooting while I talk to Coach Eric for a minute," I say. I'm thinking from a concerned mother's perspective now. "What about the guards you already have?"

"What about them" Coach Eric asks.

"Jealousy comes to mind," I say. "I don't want to worry about my sons being jumped or given a hard time because someone has to divide their playtime with them."

"My starting guards graduated last year," Coach Eric says. "Here at this school we don't have a lot of players come out which is why you see mainly forwards and centers. They'll be fine."

"I'm willing to work with you on this, but I have to ask for a small favor," I say.

"Anything," Coach Eric says.

"They have a sister around the same age as them," I say. "If they're playing on this team, I need her to be able to join the cheerleading and dance team," I continue. "Here. I'm not going from middle school to high school. They either all participating in athletics here, or I'll have to make them play middle school ball."

11

"I'll see what I can do," Coach Eric says.

On the car ride home I interrogate the boys. "Why didn't you guys tell me you wanted to play ball?" I ask.

"We didn't know we could play on the high school team," Justin says. "We've watched enough games at our school to know we would get worse playing with them."

"Oh I see. You guys think you're too good to play with kids your age?" I ask.

"No Mom," Josiah says. I'm laughing because I already know what's he's about to say and he's laughing as he says it because he knows I can read his mind. "We don't think we're too good to play with kids our age. We know we're too good to play with them"

"And we're not being cocky or conceited either Mom," Justin says. "We never told anyone. We kept it to ourselves and were just going to wait until we got in high school to play."

"So you know we gone have to change our strategy with everything right?" I ask.

The kids want to act, sing and dance. The plan was for them to stay in public school for the first half of this school year. During that time we would build our craft by taking dance classes, writing and completing a few songs as well as shoot a few web shows.

With the boys now joining the basketball team, our time is going to be cut very short. I don't like to leave them unchaperoned. I need to be at the practices and games or a friend of mines does. I'm not trusting someone I don't have a relationship with to watch my kids. I don't care if all my kids are doing is running up and down a gym with a few coaches watching them.

But back to my family's original strategy. The second half of the year, and for the duration of their education, the plan was for me to homeschool them so they can devote their time to pursuing their careers. We would release whatever we had completed

during that time and they would be free to do interviews and appearances if someone asked them to.

I don't care that we have to create a new game plan because what I want to do won't be effected. I write when they're at school. I plan to have two more books under my belt before the New Year. It's just the kids that will have to adjust.

Now that the boys are playing basketball, they will have to stay in public school longer.

When the boys walk through the door, Charise has jokes. "So you guys think y'all they stuff because y'all can hand with the big boys?" Her and her sisters laugh.

I take a shower and was planning to have a family meeting until I look at my boys who have yet to bathe after all that sweating. "Get in the tub," I say. When they finish, the kids get comfortable in my room. I let them know everything that's going on with the boys and basketball and see what their input is.

"Will we still be able to take dance classes?" Lanice asks.

"Yes," I say. "Just not as many because the boys will have games on the weekends. Our schedules are about to be tight."

"Do they have to play the whole season Mommy?" Stacey asks.

"Yes. They have to play the whole season," I say. "I'm not raising any quitters. If you start it, You're going to finish it."

"Can you homeschool us after the season is over?" Josiah asks.

I do a little research on my computer and smile at him. "Yes," I say. "But I don't think you guys are understanding that now because our schedule is tight, we won't have a lot of time to shoot or record anything. We're not going to have everything finished that we want to put out, so maybe you should just stay in public school the whole year."

"I think we should still be homeschooled when they finish," Alisa says. "That way we can catch up on the things we're not going to get done." She sounds sad.

"You mean when you, Josiah and Justin finish," I say.

She has no clue what I'm talking about.

"I talked to their coach," I say. "I told him if the boys were playing on his team, I wanted you to dance with the dance team and cheer for them as well."

Alisa's smiling now.

"Aww," Lanice and Charise whine.

"Girls I don't think that man is going to have enough pull to get all three of you on a high school cheerleading and dance team. Do you guys want to cheerlead for your school?" I ask hoping they say no. It's bad enough I had someone change their age on their birth certificate so they could get through school faster. I taught my kids at home for a while so they're definitely not behind.

"No. We'll just take the dance classes," Charise says.

So the new plan is to take them out of public school once the boy's season ends. While it's going on we'll record on the free days we will have and take dance classes. We'll complete as many projects as we can.

This should be fun. I'm excited to watch my boys compete at the Varsity level.

Chapter 5

One exciting day is followed by another one.

It's our family night. Lots of games, junk food and laughs. We play charades, catergory games, and a card game Bianca made up called Pick Granny.

Pick Granny is comical because it's obvious when Bianca and Stacey have the Granny card. They get too excited and start smiling and laughing when someone's about to pull it from them. They even try to stick the card out they want the person to pick and shift their hands a little when someone goes for a car after the Granny. They're so cute.

Family night is the only night I allow the kids to OD on junk. Chips and dip, candy, sodas, juices, cookies, just name it. We usually demolish it all before the night is over. Stacey is doing a little too much though. She's already eating so much that her jaws are moving real slow and s he looks tired.

"Stacey slow down," I say. "You don't have to eat it all tonight. You can eat some tomorrow. It's okay to be full."

"I'm not full," Stacey says like she just got done running a marathon. She's breathing hard.

Alisa is putting Lanice and Charise's hair in a ponytail. They love to be close to their big sister. They admire her The staff always tells me how popular Allisa is amongst everyone including the eight graders at school. Josiah and Justin are just as popular. The staff tells me they hear girls discussing them all the time. I know they're worried my kids will wind up pregnant soon considering how young I had them. My kids are the *'it'* kids at Python Middle School.

I turn some music on and we do a soul train line. I hate dancing with these kids because I look like an amateur dancing with pros. My kids get down. Especially Bianca and Stacey. I guess because they're so little they make anything look a lot cuter.

Me, Stacey and Justin go to the kitchen to refill our cups.

While I'm pouring my soda I hear something drop on the floor behind me. I turn around and Stacey is regurgitating small drops of what looks like chips and dip. The drops are getting bigger and bigger. Every time they do, Justin and I take a step back. Next thing we know, Stacey is throwing up heavily. We take more steps back and laugh. My other kids come to see what all the fuss is about. Josiah cleans it up. Stacey's crying.

"I told you to slow down," I say. "Come with me so ic an put you in the tub." Stacey looks so helpless right now. "I thought you weren't full?"

"I'm not," Stacey says when I grab a towel for her. "I'm still hungry."

I make her a plate of lasagna and pasta I made from scratch that's topped with feta cheese. It's bomb. I hope we have leftovers. The kids sometimes wake up before me and eat them all. I think I will put a plate aside tonight.

We end the night with a movie.

While the kids sleep, I pick up the mess they made.

Bianca wakes up while I'm in the kitchen pouring more to drink.

"Mommy I can't sleep," Bianca says.

"Okay. Sit down on the couch," I say. "You can stay up with me."

"Mommy you want help?' Bianca asks.

"If you want," I say.

My little munchkin helps me clean up the plates and cups and helps me put the leftover food away.

I don't forget to set me a plate aside.

Chapter 6

Josiah celebrates his twelfth birthday at a race car track place. He asked me to leave Bianca and Stacey at the house with Mya so I could have a complete unbothered time with him. That was a great idea. I feel full of life and scared at the same time while Josiah drives me around. He has yet to make one turn without hitting someone. I'm getting whiplash.

"I just know you gone have better driving skills in a real car right?" I ask. He purposely runs into another car and says sure.

Afterwards we go out to eat at a buffet. The same friends that came to the race car track meet us there.

I'm really enjoying watching my kids interact with their friends.

Alisa is really *Ms. Popularity.* Her friends look at her with admiration while she talks to them about how much she loves to dance. My boys are talking to their friends about some new video games that are coming out. Charise and Lanice are sitting next to me saying they want to celebrate their birthdays at a skating rink.

After everyone has eaten, we sing happy birthday to Josiah. There's three round cakes with his name on them and candles as well. They all have a different amount of candles. The one I brought, for sure has fourteen. His friends buy him things all the time.

When Josiah was five he shared his party with his friend whose birthday is around the same day as his. I had them share a cake and he got upset because his friend blew out the candles before he did. Ever since then, my kid's don't share parties anymore.

After the candles are put out, the birthday boy cuts the first slices on his cakes. His friends are snapping pictures and documenting this beautiful day.

I take my kids to see a late night movie, then we head home.

The first thing I do is flat iron Bianca's hair in my room. Alisa and Stacey are in my bed watching TV.

"Thanks for taking us out today," Josiah comes in and says.

"No problem. Happy Birthday son," I say. He kisses my forehead and goes to his room.

"Mommy Josiah is twelve now?" Bianca asks.

"Yes. And I want you to look real nice for your handsome brother's second party tomorrow," I say.

"Are we going to have two parties too Mommy?" Bianca asks.

"Yes. When you get older," I say. I really hope she forgets I said that. "You're beautiful every day but I want you to look princess beautiful tomorrow for your brother. You want Josiah's friends to see how cute their little sister is right?"

"Yes," Bianca says.

Alisa leaves my mom with an attitude and slams her room door. I check on her and she's in her bed crying.

"What's wrong Alisa?" I ask standing by the door. She shakes her head indicating nothing which is a lie. I get in the bed with her. "I can't help you if you don't know what's bothering you," I say.

"You're talking to Bianca like she's your only girl," Alisa says. "And sometimes you act like you only care about the boys."

I wrap my arms around her. "You know I love you," I say. "I'm only talking about the boys because that's who Bianca spends most of her time with out of my oldest. If I was doing Lanice and Charise's hair I would've talked about you." I kiss her cheek. "Alisa, Mommy loves you. Don't be like this. I love you just as much as those knuckle heads in there. Can you give me a hug?" She gives me a hug. I take her hand and lead her back to my room. I continue to do Bianca's hair.

"Mommy you want me to grab the other flat iron and do Stacey's?" Alisa asks. I tell her yes. I feel so bad making her cry.

I love all my kids equally. I never want them to think I favor any of them over the other.

The next day I barbeque at the park so Bianca and Stacey can celebrate with Josiah. They invited kids from school. Alisa's sitting on the steps on the playground and her girls are playing in her hair and looking at her with admiration. Some of Alisa's friends can't stop looking at Justin and Josiah.

Josiah comes over to get a burger. "Mom you doing okay?" he asks.

"Yes. Are you having fun?" I ask.

"Yes. Thank you," Josiah says. Bianca and Stacey give him a hug.

"Josiah you're twelve years old now?" Stacey asks.

"Yes. I'm a man," Josiah says.

I laugh.

"Boy you aren't anywhere close to being a man," I say.

Josiah flexes his muscles.

"Josiah you're about to go by your friends?" Stacey asks. He nods his head while chewing his burger.

"Go by Mom?" Bianca asks him.

"No. Come by me," Josiah says. He eats and watches Bianca and Stacey play on the jungle gym. I want to shed a tear. I love that my kids are so close. My son could've easily said he wanted to just spend time with his friends today and not his sisters, but he's taking some of his time to show his baby sister's that he loves them. I love my son so much.

I love all of my kids. I can't believe my son is already twelve. Time is really flying by. I feel like just yesterday I was working my behind off to get out of my mother's house. And here I am today enjoying peace and happiness and reaping the benefits of my hard work.

It's so beautiful out here. The sun is shining, the kids are laughing and having fun, the birds are chirping, there's a nice breeze, and most importantly, my inner self is at complete peace.

When we get home, I call Josiah in my room. "Did you enjoy your birthday? I ask him. He says yes. I love to hear him say it. "Is Mommy still doing a great job of making you happy?" He says yes.

"You always make me happy, Mom," Josiah says. "Even when it's not my birthday." I give him a hug and got to sleep. These last two days have been tiring. I sleep gracefully knowing my son enjoyed his birthday weekend.

I have the best feeling in the world which is my kids enjoying their life and appreciating the things I do for them.

Chapter 7

Coach Eric hold tryouts. The same people the boys scrimmaged against are the ones trying out, and the same ones that make the team. So pretty much he held tryouts as a part of doing his job.

I work hard to stay awake at the boys practice. I grab some chips out the vending machine to snack on with the coffee I brought with me.

The boys take a water break in the middle of practice. Justin runs over to me, kisses me on the forehead and says he loves me.

"You almost done?" I ask.

"Yes. Another hour and a half," Justin says and laughs as I stare at him looking exhausted. I feel like it's already been two hours. He kisses my forehead again and runs back on the court.

I'm sitting here enjoying my chips and my kids doing what they love. At the same time I'm trying to make sure I have my thoughts together for my book seminar tomorrow night. However I can't focus for too long because the girls behind me keep talking louder and louder. It's like they want me to hear what they're saying so I tune completely into them.

"She's ugly," one girl says. "Her flat iron is terrible."

"Just like her body," another girl says and a bunch of girls laugh.

"She can't compete with me," the girl that said *she's ugly* says.

I take a look around me. I don't know these girls. They can't be talking about me.

"Yea we're talking about you sitting right in front of us," the girl that she *she's ugly* says. This little blonder girl has a nasty attitude and tone. "Once he sees me he'll forget all about her," she says to her friends.

I'm laughing. I'm not taking these young ass girls serious.

"Ugly bitch," the blonde girl says. "She shouldn't have bene allowed in here. Isn't there a sign that says no uglies allowed

outside?"

"I think we should make one," another girl says.

The girls get up and leave.

When they pass me walking down the bleachers, the blonde looks at me and says, "Go to hell already."

Whatever with these immature kids. I'll write a book about them one day.

Chapter 8

There's over thirty people at the community center here to listen to me speak about my book <u>Behind the Cover.</u> It's about a man named Joe, who tells his tory in all of his books. Joe writes according to the things he encounters in life but no one knows. He creates a story about everyone that played a bad role in his life that he no longer talks to. What makes it more interesting is when one of Joe's friends, Don, catches onto it, Joe purposely has people break into Don' house and steal his things. Joe makes sure to witness his friend's anger by stopping by to console him. Then he turns around and writes a story about how he hired people to ruin Don's house and because he was upset that Don wrote a story about his own brother, but didn't want Joe to write about him.

I look sharp in my grey skirt set business suit as I greet everyone.

"Good evening everyone," I say. "Thanks for coming out. I don't want to keep you guys too long so let's get straight into <u>Behind the Cover.</u> What many of you probably don't know is I walked around downtown LA for two weeks just to come up with some crazy characters that my lead Joe could write about. I chose to go there because that's where I always saw a lot of crazy people."

"I observed people from head to toe," I continue. "I watched how they walked, talked and interacted with others while I sat at a table pretending to read a newspaper."

I think a lot of authors come up with good ideas by just simply sitting in a public atmosphere.

"One day a homeless man came in a store when I was in the checkout line," I say. "He took some chips, ate them in the store, then left only to find that the police were at the door. He tried to run but was caught. I took that story and ran with it."

I tell everyone how I came up with all my characters

personalities, looks, and where and why I wanted Joe to encounter them. I tell them about my brainstorming process and conclude with writing tips and the importance of not rushing anything.

Now the floors open for questions.

"How did you come up with this book?" a woman asks.

"For a long time I contemplated writing books about all the weird psycho, and whackos I've met since I've been in California, but decided that putting them in print form would cause me to remember them for the rest of my life. My hope is to forget them so I created Joe and got some ideas traveling through town. I could never write a book describing the real 'cartoon characters' I met in life. I know they're crazy selves will track me down and try to hurt me if they ever took the time to read the book."

"How long did it take you to write this?" a woman in the back asks.

"Two months," I say. Everyone looks shocked. "Let me tell you guys, if you have a story drawn out in your mind and you already know all the points you want to hit, as long as you discipline yourself to get a certain amount down on paper a day, you can finish a book in a month is you want to."

"Is there going to be a sequel to the story?" a teenage girl asks.

"No," I say. I don't plan on writing sequels to any of my books.

I tackle a subject and move on. I don't want to write about the same topic twice.

As soon as I pull up to my house, my girls come out. I don't have any time to relax before their dance class. Thankfully it's only an hour. I'm very impressed. They all pick up the choreography fast and put their own personalities into it. The choreographer is amazed at Bianca and Stacey. He has someone recording it, so I give him my email so I can have a link to the

video. The girls beg me to take another class with a different instructor so we switch rooms and stay another hour.

When I get home, I go straight to my bed. The only thing I take off is my heels. I'm going to be sure to put some emergency shoes in my car next time. My heels have my feet crying.

Alisa hops in the bed with me and rests her head on my back.

"Alisa baby go in your room," I say.

"But I want to be close to my mommy. I love you so much," Alisa says kissing my forehead repeatedly.

"Go take a shower or something," I say.

"I can't. they're all occupied," Alisa says.

"You excited to perform at the game on Friday?" I ask.

"I am," Alisa says. ""I can't wait. Make sure you record it okay Mommy?"

"Of course," I say. She hold me tighter.

It's hard to believe this is the same child that thought she heard me talking bad about her a few years ago. Alisa had the story all wrong.

There's a character on this show I watch with the same name as her. The character thought she was this top notch woman and she always treated people like they were beneath her. One day Alisa must've been standing by my door while I was on the phone with a friend and listened to me bash the woman completely. I mean I was going in saying stuff like: *people like her don't' deserve to live. I hope I never meet someone like her. She's ugly internally so externally she's painful to look at.* I mean I said a lot of stuff. My precious little daughter heard, but didn't tell me up front. Instead, that same night she took a jump rope and tried to hand herself. Her brothers and sisters were furious when she told them why she tried to kill herself so for an entire month they gave me pure hell. Talked back, hid my stuff, stole money from me, and called me every derogatory name they could think of. They even locked me out the house for a few minutes one day.

It wasn't until I called the cops, to give my kids a scare that I would get rid of them, that everything was revealed. Unfortunately for them I didn't take kind to Bianca almost dying because when I was locked out the house she was inside choking on her candy. I'm thankful I got in before she lost all her breath. I wanted to lay hands on all my kids, but instead I asked Mya to watch them and stayed at a hotel with Bianca and Stacey until I cooled off.

When I got back, me and the kids had serious conversation. They all apologized to me as well as Biance. They vowed to never disrespect me again and always open their mouths if something bothered them. Josiah took it the hardest that Bianca almost died. They became really close when I brought her back home form the hotel. She started screaming one day because her head was stuck behind his bunk bed and he rushed put the bathroom butt naked to help her get it out.

It was a setback for us, but we are closer than ever after the situation with Alisa and scare of losing Bianca. No one knows about the situation except us, and that' show we plan to keep it.

Alisa is falling asleep on my back. "Cut the light off and shut the door," I tell her. She does as she's told.

"Mommy do you think I'm pretty?" Alisa asks.

"Of course I do," I say. "Don't' ask me questions you already know the answer to. I think all of my girls are perfect." Alisa knows she's gorgeous. Completely flawless at that. Sometimes my kids just want to be babied. They like to be up under me and act like babies at times. I guess sometimes they just want to hear me say those words despite me letting hem know quite often. Whatever the case, I'm happy I could put her to sleep with those kind words being the last ones she heard.

We both knock out.

Chapter 9

It's game time at Floyd High School. The gym is crowded and packed. I have Charise save my seat while I go get some cheese fries. There's still ten minutes before jump ball. The girls and I tear the fries up. I have Charise go get another batch since she ate most of them and she said she didn't want none.

The clock runs out and it's game time. I can't believe my eyes. Josiah is starting. Jump ball goes up and the other team has possession. Josiah hops in the passing lane, steals the ball, and scores the first points of the game.

I see *'little miss blondie'* with the attitude problem across the court. I'm not going to say anything to my girls about what she said because I don't want them getting upset. They'll knock the life out the girl and her crew if they found out what they were saying about their mama. I'm here for my sons anyways. I'm not trying to start any mess. I'm grown.

Josiah is showing out. Ten points in the first three minutes of the game off steals alone. Half way through the first quarter Justin subs in for him.

"Damn. It's two of them," a man going for the opponent's team says. He's upset, but some people laugh. Me and my kids are some of them.

Justin shows out just like his brother. They're just too quick with everything. They're up twenty points at the end of the first quarter. The entire crowd is in shock at what they're witnessing.

"Aye, how old are they?" the same upset man yells.

"Don't worry about it," Bianca turns around and says. I'm still laughing so I don't turn around.

It's half time now. Alisa takes the court with her dance team and tears it up. She mastered the choreography and she looks good doing it.

Bianca is cracking me up. She's recording with Alisa's phone and only recording Alisa. She has it zoomed in so only Alisa fits

on the screen and follows her left and right.

Bianca keeps twisting her little body left and right. I'm smiling so hard. I'm recording with my phone. I have the entire team on my screen so I can capture all the formations and appreciate the entire routine the coach took time out to come up with. My little girl is doing so good for her first Varsity performance.

Fourth quarter rolls around and Floyd's students start chanting for the coach to put Justin and Josiah in at the same time. He doesn't. He swaps them out the entire game.

We win by sixty-five points. This crowd can't believe what they just watched. They haven't even moved yet to exit out. Everyone's staring at my boys to see who they're here with.

Unfortunately the girls and I are meeting them in the car.

Chapter 10

Today is Lanice's birthday. She has a few of her friends meet us at the skating rink. I'm sitting at a table with Bianca and Stacey eating nachos and there's this girl staring at me. I can see her out my peripheral visions. I turn to her and she's doing exactly what I thought she was: staring at my bushy eyebrows looking upset. I try not to let it bother me in front of Bianca and Stacey who are eating with me. I let it go and continue to have a good time.

When we get home the kids pull up their computers to upload their photos. I shed tears when Charise uploads one of me, Bianca and Stacey smiling, and the girl that was staring at my bushy eyebrows is in the background still staring. I'm embarrassed.

"It's okay Mom. She's just a stupid kid," Charise says.

I can hear the frustration in her voice. She closes her computer and gives me a hug. I know the kids hate that I have to go through this constantly. I'm so embarrassed that they have to deal with people staring at what makes me different than the average human being. I know like everyone else that has a parent that has features different from what a normal body is considered, that they hate seeing people stare at their mom in a rude heartless way. I know they just wish I had better looking eyebrows. Then they wouldn't have to worry about extras in the background ruining their photos of me.

But the fact is, I don't have cute eyebrows. I'm different.

I could get surgery, but I don't want to. I want to just accepts the way I was born. I want to show people that they don't have to be like everybody else. We all don't have to look the same. I want to inspire people that are born different to keep moving forward and don't pay the world any attention.

I'm lying. Just don't look at me. Different. We need to enhance the way we were made. We're not here to all be the same.

The kids stay up all night and post pictures of the party on their accounts.

I go to bed.

My head hurts.

Chapter 11

After only three games under the boy's belts, I'm contacted for the boys to appear in a shoe commercial.

It's tomorrow.

I just got the email today. I didn't know the commercial process was so fast. They didn't give me any time to think. The girls are going to have to miss dance class.

The boys, Alisa and I arrive at the commercial shoot, which is on an outdoor basketball court. There's these tall ass men here. I'm assuming they're professional players. Me and Alisa sit at a distance and watch the cameras pick up the boys hit a few shots in what are called *Bomb Zone Shoes*.

The boys play a slow game up and down the court a few times. It looks like Josiah has a speaking part too.

When they finish, someone hands my boys an envelope and we head out.

Josiah's eyes are wide open when he pulls out his cash in the car.

"How much is it?" I ask.

"Two thousand," Josiah says. "A piece."

"I could get used to this," Justin says.

They're getting a lot of recognition and attention now. I don't mind them gaining a spotlight, but I mind it being cast on me. I don't want fame. Only thing I'm glad about when it comes to them having a big audience is my books are selling more.

"What was that man talking to you about?" I ask referring to the tall man that stopped the boys while I got in the car.

"He was just saying how talented we are and how impressed he was with our skills," Josiah says.

"I think it's tight he's only twenty-three," Justin says. "We'll be playing with him one day."

After that long commercial shoot, all I want to do is sleep, but someone is tapping on the wall from Alisa, Charise and Lanice's

room.

"Girls come here!" I yell. "Who's doing all that tapping on the wall?"

"Lanice," Charise quickly says.

"That wasn't me. It was Alisa," Lanice says.

"It was both of you," I say.

"I wasn't tapping on the wall Mom," Alisa says. "They were going back and forth trying to make the same beat."

"Everybody said something different," I say frustrated. "Two people are lying. And I think one is you Lanice because you're the one always making stuff up when things don't go your way or you don't want to get punished."

Most people only have to listen to two sides of a story and here I am listening to three. On a real bad day I'll have five different sides.

"Stop," before I can say beating on the wall I take a deep breath and try to relax while Lanice is walking out the room. I quickly get out my bed, grab her shirt and turn her around. "I am tired of you walking away from me when I'm talking to you."

"I didn't know you had more to say," Lanice whines. "I thought you were finished."

"I don't know who it is, but you better stop beating on the wall," I say. "It's not an instrument and people are trying to go to sleep. Now you can go to your room."

As soon as they get in their room they start arguing. I'm really upset now. Charise is saying Alisa and Lanice know it was them making all the noise, and it probably was because they're laughing and she's angry. I'm not tripping because they all have their moments like this. There's been days when Charise was the one laughing and they were upset after I got done fussing.

"Everybody go to bed," I say.

I lay down with Charise. I hate seeing my kids in tears no matter what the situation. Lanice and Alisa are still chuckling under their covers. I know they're sending text messages back

and forth. I kiss Charise on her forehead.

"I know y'all better quiet down and put them message alerts on silent," I say.

We have a nice family but these are kids just like everyone else's. They have their moments.

Charise might be over this tomorrow.

Chapter 12

My family gets invited to make an appearance on the *King Denton Show.* It's not a big time talk show but it gets a pretty decent audience.

The focus is on Josiah and Justin, but Denton's so nosy to figure out who's responsible and related to these two handsome boys, so he wants my entire family sitting with them.

Denton asks the boys a series of questions about their natural talent and playing on the high school level at such young ages.

"I love playing with older kids," Josiah says. "I love being challenged."

"We just love to play," Justin says. "We don't care who we're playing with. We've been playing around with basketballs since we were two. I think that's why it comes so easy to us."

"A lot of kids have had balls in their hands since they were two," Denton says. "But none of them are as good as you two."

The boys say thank you.

"So Mom, you look really good," Denton continues. "How old are you and when did you have your kids?"

I give him all the answers and hold my composure as the crowd stares at me in disbelief.

I told y'all I hate when people give me those shocked stress and gasps because of how young I look and how many kids I have at my age.

The interview is going okay. I enjoy myself until I see this bitch, excuse me, girl Vayda, sitting in the audience. I used to love shit girl to death. She was my favorite living beauty. But I learned who she was long ago.

When I first came to California, I was out a lot. I hired a caretake while I was out getting familiar with the area.

One day I went out to eat and sat outside next to the window to enjoy my food. Okay. Sound innocent enough. The next day in my timeline on my *ChitChatFam* account there was a picture of

me sitting outside that window enjoying my food and Vayda pointing to my bushy eyebrows looking disgusted. She had someone take the picture and she posted it to her millions of fans. After that picture came a video of her pretending to almost throw up, then the camera panning to my eyebrows.

The comments were so mean. The video had thousands of likes and reposts.

I cried night after night because of her. I lost days of sleep. it was just awful. It took me a couple weeks to get over it. There she was posting hurtful stuff about me, and there I was deleting all the nice beautiful pictures of her from my account.

I blocked her after that. I didn't want to see anything she was doing or hear anything about her. I wanted her to turn into a ghost.

I still do.

It's crazy how that worked out. I wanted to work with Vayda one day on a film I hope to write eventually, but forget that. My favorite beauty is evil-spirited. Her heart is all messed up.

It kills me how she's always posting about being beautiful internally and externally but doesn't possess beauty anywhere in my eyes. I hate those lying girls that put themselves out there to be something they're not.

Truth be told, I don't really even think Vayda's a great actress. If we were to work together, I'd make her get a coach before she ruined my project like so many other projects she's ruined. She's one of those women that are too stupid to see that everyone tells her what she wants to hear to get in her pants.

Who in their right mind would tell someone they desperately want to sleep with that they can't act? The sad thing to me is people really have this girl thinking she's worthy of an acting award. Yes. That's how much people feed her ego. There's top notch actresses that have countless awards that people don't consistently keep telling them the obvious which is that they're talented. Somebody like Vayda, who is pure awful unless she's

playing a tramp and gold digger, which is what everyone thinks of her in real life, people consistently tell her she's good knowing she's not.

I mean it's really disgusting when I see her out smiling and laughing knowing that her mind is full of lies that her dumb self believes.

I'm probably just saying all this because I can't stand her because she scarred me, but I don't care. I'll hate on a mean girl day in and day out. Vayda means nothing to me anymore. She's cruel and pathetic.

But anyways. After I started getting recognition and all types of awards for my writing, Vayda deleted the heartless posts. A day after she did, I was contacted by a famous talk show host that I knew she worked with on a television show.

I really waned to go because I loved the host. She played in one of my favorite movies. But I already knew what she was going to do. My discernment told me she would invite Vayda. I didn't want to see her. I wasn't going to let her off the hook that easy. Vayda would've sat down with me and acted real nice, stared into my eyes and not my eyebrows, proved to the world that she can be comfortable around people that *have* bushy eyebrows, then anyone that saw her ugly posts about me would forget about how heartless she was.

I couldn't let her off the hook that easy.

I ignored the email I received.

A week after not responding to going on the show, Vayda uploaded a picture kissing my forehead. I was way too furious and still am at what she did to me to get happy over the post.

Of all the people in the world, she was in the top five that I hoped would never hurt my feelings. She actually read a few of my books and promoted them, but I don't care.

People like to say I have an attitude problem because I don't want to look at them after I catch them staring at my eyebrows like I'm disgusting. But that's not the case. I don't see it that way

at all. I look at it as not taking a chance on seeing the same hurtful facials again.

It's bad enough the first time I witnessed the look it plays over and over again in my head, but it's painful to look at people that look at me like I shouldn't be a human in the eyes again.

How can people that stare at me mean be mad at me when I don't want to look at them again instead of checking themselves because they are the ones staring at people that are born different weird and making our lives harder?

If I don't want to look at those people again, they need to just respect it.

Okay. I'm done.

Let me get out my feelings.

But not before I let you know I had the perfect plan to get Vayda back for what she did to me. I don't want to talk about it thought because I no longer have what I need.

Okay, back to the King Denton interview.

For some reason Vayda is winking at one of my kids. But I can't tell which one. I never told the kids I didn't like her. They don't even know she has evil traits to her. I was the only person with a different body feature that she ever picked on, and by the time my kids got of age, she had already deleted the posts. My kids aren't the type to look up bad posts on people.

If they're fans of Vayda they only see what she's posting these days. And these days she's not making the mistake of joking about the way someone was born because she did that to me, and now I'm successful and she loves my writing ability.

I'm having a hard time figuring out why she's here. I hope not to approach me backstage.

Soon as the interviews done, me and the kids head straight to the car. We don't have time to talk to anyone.

Some girls walk in front of us and Josiah smiles at them. Justin doesn't. I know exactly why.

"You gone tell me who she is when we get home," I whisper

to Justin.

When Justin gets out the show, I'm sitting on his bed waiting for him.

"Mom," Justin smiles.

"Come on son," I say. "Sit next to me. Tell Mommy who she is."

"She goes to Terrance D. Middle School," Justin says.

"So how did you meet her if you don't go to school with her?" I ask. "I see you over there smiling Josiah."

"She came to a few of my practices and games," Justin says.

"Who approached who?" I ask.

"She dropped her books and I helped her pick them up," Justin says.

Josiah's laughing and shaking his head. I know he's thinking the same thing I am. Whoever the girl is knew exactly what she was doing. She wanted Justin. She doesn't even go to a school that's close to Floyd yet her young self was up there.

"What's her name?" I ask.

"Grace," Justin says.

"Well you better bring Grace by so I can meet her one day," I say.

Some glass shatters.

"What was that?!" I yell.

Stacey is crying over the glass cup she dropped. She knows I don't allow her or Bianca to carry around any type of glass. I don't believe in hitting my kids so I send her to bed early.

There's been days when I thought about putting a belt on my kid's behinds, but I just couldn't bring myself to do it. My mother never hit me so maybe that's why I can't bring myself to hit them.

I love my kids too much to put them in physical pain.

"Mommy you upset?" Stacey cries as I tuck her in.

"Yes," I honestly say. "Don't touch my glass cups again."

Justin cleans up the glass for me. .

38

I go in my room and type in me and Vayda's name on my *ChitChatFam*. The pictures and video she created making a mockery of me like it's okay to make jokes about the way people were created, are still the top thing that comes up when searching our names together. That's why she was so fixed on trying to get me in the same place as her for that interview. Both of us on a huge daytime talk show together would surely take over the top spot when typing our names in together eventually.

If I wouldn't have garnered attention from my books, she would have never taken the posts down because no one would care about me. It wasn't until she realized I was a popular writer and some of the people she idolized were fans of mine that she took down those posts.

That's ridiculous to me.

I shouldn't have to be famous for Vayda to be kind and care about my feelings. By the time she did, too many people already had the posts copied. They're never going away. Some of her fans joked about the pictures and other ones let her know how unkind she was, but it still took for her to realize I was gaining a little popularity to leave me alone and take the photos down.

I get on my *FriendSpot* account and I have a comment from a page titled I love Leah that says: *Check it out* Leah with a link to a photo. I click it needing to see some posts from peple that love me. Instead there's a bunch of pictures similar to the one Vayda did disrespecting the way I look. The only difference is these are photo-shopped pictures of people making rude faces on a blown-up image of my face to look at my eyebrows. There's even Vayda's creations on the page as well.

I can't stand when childish people post a nice comment to lead you to a mean page.

I close out the account and cry myself to sleep.

Chapter 13

I need a night on the town. I hit up Mya and she's down to go, but I need to find a sitter. I want to hit my forehead when it dawns on me that the boys are playing with high school kids. It took too long to think of that.

"Josiah, who on your team is eighteen years old?" I ask.

"Evan and James are," Josiah says.

"See if one of them can come watch y'all tonight and I'll pay them," I say.

Evan arrives promptly at ten.

Mya and I are just about ready. Alisa is flat ironing the back of my hair.

"I'm done Mommy," Alisa says.

"Thank you. Have Evan come here," I say.

I sent for Evan but Justin and Josiah are in my face too. I know they don't like that their teammate loves staring at me.

"Don't be nervous," I say. "I know they're young but they're well-behaved. They ate already, but if for some reason they get hungry again, Alisa knows to fix them a sandwich or something. You can help yourself to whatever you want."

"Okay," Evan says.

Justin and Josiah are staring at Evan lust after my body.

When Mya and I walk towards the door, I hear the boys ask Evan in a low voice if he likes me. He quickly says no and shakes his head in a way that lets us all know he's lying.

Mya and I end up going to a club. We only stay for an hour because we're not feeling the crowd.

"Where you want to go?" Mya asks me when we pull off.

I hit up one of my male companions, Westin, and tell him to invite a friend over. We all chill in Westin's bedroom.

Me and Westin are cuddled up on the bed, and his friend Q and Mya are sitting on the couch he has in the corner.

"So what you been doin' all night?" Westin asks.

"Nothing," I say. "We hit up a club, but it was whack so we left."

"Oh, so I'm your last option?" Westin asks.

"It's not even like that," I say.

"Y'all got some good?" Mya asks.

Her and Q go outside and smoke.

Me and Westin get it in. We strap up because neither of us wants anymore kids right now. He knows I have seven and he has five of his own.

I definitely need this tonight. I'm not a sexaholic or anything but I do go through droughts because I'm so busy with the kids and don't like to leave them a lot. I would invite him over but the kids are nosy. I don't want to put sex in their brains no more than the TV already has.

When we finish, Westin's curiosity kicks in while he holds me.

"So I take it you and t hat boy don't talk no more," Westin says.

He's referring to this man named Matthew I was pursuing.

"No. We don't," I say.

"Can I ask what happened?" Westin asks.

"He can't take being with a woman that's…" I can't finish the statement. It's hard for me to admit everyone can't handle the things that come with being with me.

"That's what?" Westin asks.

"Don't worry about it," I say.

I just don't want to talk about it.

Before heading to the house, me and Mya hit up a spot to eat. We went in to order but we're sitting here eating in the car.

We're both faded.

Me from alcohol.

Mya from weed.

My seat is reclined back as I eat my nachos and chicken tenders. Mya's seat is too while she eats her burger and fries.

"Don't you wish we could chill like this every night?" Mya asks.

"You can chill like this every day," I say. "I'm the one with all the kids."

"At least you got some good ones," Mya says. "Shit, I know people that got two kids, but they bad as hell and get they ass beat damn near every day. You blessed girl."

"Yea I love my kids," I say.

"And you got kids with talent. You set," Mya says.

"You crazy girl. When you gone have some?" I ask.

"Not no time soon," Mya says. "I'm renting out rooms and shit, still trying to get on my own. I wouldn't dare bring nobody in this world living like this. I don't eve have a man yet to plan nothing out."

"He'll come girl," I say. "He'll come. Don't settle for anyone. Make sure he's worth your time."

"You ain't got to tell me," Mya says. "Damn near everyone I know is with someone they don't want to be with. It's either for the sex, the money or because they have low self-esteem."

"You mean they don't think they'll find anyone else?" I ask.

"Yes," Mya says. "They'd rather get they ass beat and get talked to like they ain't shit than ride solo."

"That's the world we live in," I say. "I wish we had a bottle right now to cheers to being smart independent women."

We finish eating, but I'm nowhere near tired. We drive around my old neighborhoods for a while.

Mya pulls up on the side of a street from one of my old residences.

"A car lit on fire in that alley," I say. "I swear up and down it was the son of the dude I was staying with. Boy was just off. He kept stealing from the old lady that stayed with us and she knew it but still wanted to keep paying his dad rent."

"She must've liked the dad," Mya says.

"Exactly," I say. "She thought I was so damn stupid. She said

42

her and Earl knew each other's kids. Or some shit like that. Earl's the thieve's dad. I know him and that old lady had to be fucking before they became roommates. The old lady was always complaining that Earl only smoked all day and preyed on women. She took me to church a few times then turned around and asked me to hack Earl's *ChitChatFam* account when he was out of town."

I absolutely hate when church people act holy then say something that makes me question why they go to church.

"I couldn't stand either of them," I say. "Earl kept asking me if I wore stilettos and to go out with his old ass."

"How old was he?" Mya asks.

"Sixty-three and the old layd was around fifty-eight," I say. "She got on my nerves so much. She asked too many damn questions. She always wanted to know what time Earl and his son were in the house and what time they had company. We were talking one day and she found out we both had a friend in Victorville and she asked me where my friend lived. Shit was fucking with me. I'll never make the mistake of living with two old people again."

"That bastard probably still living here," Mya says. "I should throw a rock at his window."

I love this girl.

"Girl, and let me tell you," I say. "When the old man clears his throat it sounds terrible. It's so much nasty spit stuck in his lungs. I couldn't deal with that shit. He needs to do two things: get that shit checked and stop smoking. There's no reason his throat should be making them kinds of sounds. I did not like hearing that old man ask someone if she swallowed on my way to the kitchen either. He had over some random girl that day."

"Hell no," Mya says. "Thankfully in a month I'll have enough saved up to move out and on my own. I don't even want to think about my roommates developing habits like that. Let's go though because I don't like posting up in gang territory. You know you

in the hood when all the fast food places and convenient stores got bullet proof windows at the cash registers."

"How's your mom doin'?" Mya asks.

"She alright, I guess," I say. "She call every once in a while to make sure I'm still alive, but that's it."

Again. My mom is out living the fast life. She's not thinking about anything but having a good time each day. She not focused on the past or the future. Just the second that she's living right now. I'm not upset about it. She is who she is. This is nothing new to me. I don't have time to mope around. I have seven kids to raise.

When me and Mya pull in front of my house, we chill in the car for a few more minutes.

"We need to start doing this more often," Mya says.

"Yea we do," I say. "I love my knuckle heads, but it's nice to get away from them at times. You know I appreciate you helping me out right?"

"Of course girl," Mya says. "I can't thank you enough for editing my book. That's a huge reason I was able to save up for months. I got faith that one day it will take off like yours did, then I won't have to work another day in my life."

"I hear that," I say.

"And your kids are cool," Mya says. "They go they heads on straight, they respect me, and we have fun. I don't have a problem being there for you when you need."

Mya decides to drive home instead of crash on my couch.

Everyone's sleep except Josiah who is sitting in front of the front door. He grabs his chair and puts it back in the kitchen. He really thinks he's my daddy. He rests his head on my shoulder and puts his arm around my waist while I sit on the couch. My feet hurt too bad to make it upstairs.

"I can carry you," Josiah says.

"Boy you not about to tote me up them stairs," I say. "How was it having your teammates watch you guys?"

"Good. I felt like I had a big brother," Josiah says. "I overheard Alisa saying she wants one of her teammates to watch us next time. Go ahead and tell her no."

"You crazy," I say. "since you chillin' with me, why don't you tell me something about you I don't know. Do you have a girlfriend you want to tell me about?"

"Momma I don't want no woman right now," Josiah says. "I just want to make sure you're happy."

"Aww. I love you son," I say. "Go in the kitchen and pour me some of that wine please."

I finish my glass and me and my oldest fall asleep on the couch.

Before Evan walks out the door the next evening he tells me, "You look nice today Ms. Leah."

"Thanks," I say.

"I'm not saying that because I like you," Evan says. I don't respond so before he wlks out the door he comes back and says again, "I'm not saying that because I like you." He thought I didn't hear him.

I'd have probably bit my tongue if he didn't say it a second time. But now I'm really annoyed.

"Evan, I don't want you," I say. "Now I don't know who put it in your brain that I do, but I suggest you walk on out that door before you get your little feelings hurt."

I don't understand this boy. Josiah or Justin must've gave him a hard time about the way he was looking at me last night. All them boys crazy. I mean, I know I'm not that much older than Evan, but there's nothing that young boy can do for me. He probably still growing in his private areas. I didn't mean to do him like that before the game tonight be he really tried me.

45

Chapter 14

I can't take it no more. The boys win by fifty-eight points. I mean is there any competition in the whole state? All the teams we've played so far should be ashamed.

Between basketball, Alisa's extra activities, and the girls taking dance classes, we don't have time to finish a single web show, and no one feels like writing and recording songs. I haven't even hired a beat maker yet.

Oh well. At least the kids are doing something. Me on the other hand, I'm more drained than I thought I would be. Even with them gone during the day for school, I still don't feel like writing. I just want to sleep and enjoy not having to go nowhere.

The kids extracurricular activities have me beat.

But anyways.

Tomorrow I'm letting the kids have a Christmas Eve party. They're helping decorate the inside of the house with lights.

When the Christmas Eve party starts, Mya and I sip whine while the kids relax with their friends, eat, and enjoy music. I wanted to play some Christmas songs but the kids shut that down. Rap music is playing. I don't mind.

Mya runs to her car. I shut my eyes for a few seconds and have to open them because of Justin.

"Mom," Justin says. He's smiling hard as he holds hands with a familiar looking girl. He's bringing her to me. She looks scared at what I'm about to say. And her rude ass should be.

"Mom this is Grace," Justin says.

"Hi," I say and shake her hand. She's real nervous, but she doesn't have anything to worry about. My sons been talking about her for a few months now. He really likes her so I won't tell him how she disrespected me at this practice because she thought I was his girlfriend and not his mom. I'm going to keep that to myself.

"I'll be right back," Justin says purposely leaving me with his

girlfriend.

"How are you?" I ask with a serous tone, looking at her like the rude girl she is now that my son is out of the picture.

"Good," Grace shyly says.

"Are you having fun?" I ask.

"Yes," Grace says.

I don't think she gets that I'm prolonging this conversation because I'm waiting on her to apologize.

I take a sip of my wine and rudely ask, "Are you enjoying basketball season so far?"

"I'm really sorry for what I said," Grace says.

It's about time. I just think she really likes Justin and doesn't want to lose him. She's doing what's necessary to keep her boyfriend. I don't like that. However, Christmas is tomorrow and I'm a forgiving person. I put my glass down and give her a hug.

"Don't worry about it," I whisper. "I'll keep this between me and you alright. Don't talk like that about anyone else."

Grace says okay. Justin walks outside pretending like he didn't see me hug his girlfriend.

"Go ahead and finish enjoying the party," I tell Grace.

I step outside with Mya to release some steam after talking to Grace. Of all people, my son's love interest is the rude blond girl from the basketball gym. And of all the names her rude self can have, she's named Grace.

That little girl had me hot that day at the boys practice. Only fresh air can blow some of the steam I was holding in away.

Mya's on the phone with one of her relatives. Apparently she broke one of his vases when she was a kid and he's still mad about it ten years later. I just can't with her conversation. I head back inside and check on the kids.

Charise, Lanice and Alisa are doing a routine they learned at the dance studio. I spot Justin with Grace leaned up against him. Josiah is talking to some of his teammates and friends from school. Bianca and Stacey are in the living room looking under

47

the tree for which presents have their names on them. They're picking them up trying to guess what's inside.

Around ten at night I start having the kids call their parents. It's time to go.

I wake up early, and the kids are already sitting with their presents in front of them. I also gave each of them a hundred dollars a piece and secret Santa's.

I pull my camera out and they start unwrapping. They play with their toys and new video games and try on clothes and shoes all day.

I guess we can rest the remainder of the break right? Wrong. The boys have to play in the Christmas holiday tournament. The 26th, 27th, and 29th.

They beat everyone in the tournament by forty or more.

I'm now free for a few days. All I'm doing is sleeping.

Chapter 15

I can't believe how my life has been. The boys joining one sport took up all the time. I'm mentally drained. The season doesn't end until March.

Six months out of the year dedicated to basketball is not the business for me. But hey. If they want to play then I'm going to let my babies play.

The next few weeks, the kids and I have the same agenda: basketball, cheerleading and dance.

Grace introduces me to her parents in hopes that I start to like her more, so Justin can spend time at her house. Her parents seem cool so I let him go over there from time to time without my supervision.

I chill with Grace's parents for a day and I get a vibe that I don't like. They're those parents that throw their daughters on boys they know will bring home a lot of money. It's just obvious. That would explain Grace's filthy mouth when I first met her. Her mother and father Mrs. Claire and Mr. Ron Wallace's demeanor says it all. All they want to talk about is my boys making it straight to the pros. They keep asking me if any endorsements have been offered to us and what the boys will be doing during the off season. Mr. Ron keeps saying he can help out with finding them gigs. To make things worse they keep talking about the commercial they saw the boys in. They are really on my nerves.

"I haven't been checking my email lately," I say. "I'm still trying to figure out what route I want to take. I have five other kids besides the boys that have things they want to do so I have to balance things out."

"If you need help just let me know," Mr. Ron says.

"Grace is having a party Saturday," Mrs. Claire says. "I know she'd love for the boys to come."

"Sure. I don't mind," I say. "Where's it at?"

"A hotel," Mr. Ron says. "It's her birthday. She's turning. Thirteen."

I feel like Grace knows and does a lot more than I want Justin to know and od. I know I'm overreacting though. Maybe if I didn't sit down with her parents, I would be more open to letting him go.

Meanwhile, Grace and Justin are not in our sight. I don't know where they are in this house, but I know there's no one else here.

Mrs. Claire and Mr. Ron are a trip. They don't have a problem with their daughter being alone with a boy in their house. I'm working hard not to show my uneasiness. They're kids; they're going to do things.

Believe me I know.

For some reason I think my boys love me too much to disobey my rule of not having sex until they're married or at least out of my house. I always joke with them and tell them if they get anyone pregnant I'm putting them out too. They like to play around with the 'what ifs' and ask what if they get pregnant or get someone pregnant at fourteen like I did.

I know I sound naïve thinking all my kids will go through their teenage years practicing abstinence, but I have high hopes. But if they crush, I'm at least hoping they don't have sex before they're fifteen. I really hope they make it that far.

Mr. Ron hands me a card for the party and I let him know I'll talk to the boys about it.

"Where's Justin?" I ask.

"I think they're in the den," Mrs. Claire says.

Sure enough him and Grace are in the den with the door closed.

"Y'all bet not be having sex," I tell Justin in the car.

"Mom, I'm not," Justin says.

"If you were would you tell me?" I ask.

"No," Justin laughs.

50

I'm serious as a heart attack.

"Can me and Josiah go to her party Mom?" Justin asks.

I'm slow to answer.

"Yes. You really like that little girl huh?" I ask.

Justin's smile says it all.

"Make sure you get to know her and her parents a little better before you get too attached and start developing more feelings than you already have for her," I say. "Have you talked to her parents before?"

"No," Justin says. "Do you like them?"

"Yea. They're okay," I lie.

I don't want to put a glitch in his eyes towards Grace because of her parents, even though I know she's on the gold digging end.

"I just can't be around them too long," I say. "They actually had kids at an appropriate age so we have a good difference between us. I'm not saying I can't be around people that are twenty years older than me, but these particular ones I can't."

"Why?" Justin laughs.

"Son, they just not my type of people," I say.

While Justin's young I'm gone let him learn to feel people out for himself. What are the odds he's still with this girl by the time he's fifteen? Not high at all. There's gone be some girls that treat Grace exactly like she did me and even worse considering the boys have a little fame now. She gone get a run for her money.

But whatever for right now. My son likes her. I don't want to be the reason they fall apart if she is the one.

Chapter 16

I drop Josiah and Justin off at the hotel party when Saturday arrives. The Wallace's went all out for numero thirteen.

This is the biggest suite I've ever been in. There's caterers and the place loos like it was professionally decorated.

I speak to the Wallace's before I head out.

"I'll be back at eleven," I say.

"Okay. See you then," Mrs. Claire says.

"Alright boys. Have a good time," I say.

"Bye Momma," Justin and Josiah say.

They give me a kiss on the cheek and I head home.

I walk into an upset Bianca when I walk in my house.

"Mom, Lanice is making us watch the movie on that small square on the guide channel because she can't get her way," Bianca says.

Lanice looks guilty as hell looking at me. She looke like her feelings are hurt. I don't feel like dealing with this. I walk up the stairs.

"You not gone do nothing?" Bianca asks frustrated.

I answer her by shutting my room door.

Mya's propped up on my bed eating fruit.

"What time the party over?" Mya asks.

"Twelve," I say. "But I'm getting them earlier than that."

I sit back on the bed with her and eat a few pineapples.

"What's going on with the kids downstairs?" I ask.

"Lanice set the timer for a show but everyone else was already down there watching something else and told her not to change it," Mya says. "They all got a TV in they rooms right?"

"Yea girl which is why I didn't pay Bianca no mind," I say.

"You know I ran into Matt when I stopped to get gas?" Mya asks.

My stomach just turned. I lost my appetite. I really don't want to hear this man's name again.

"He asked about you," Mya says. "You never did tell me what happened."

"Don't worry about it," I say. "I don't want to talk about him."

I don't even want to remember him. He's the reason I just hook up with people now. I don't pursue anyone.

Now I'm not sure if this is a fact or what not, but I'm pretty sure it is. Once someone made a collage of what they thought me and Matt's kids would come out like if we ever had any together. Ever since those pictures spread around, he's been ignoring my calls.

Matt made me just as angry as this little girl that got caught staring at my eyebrows and brought me a gift the next day as an 'I'm sorry'.

I don't like guilt gifts and I sure as heck don't want anything to remind me of the person that looked at me in a way that I don't like. I wanted to tell the little girl to keep the gift but too many people were around so I took it, then put it in the dumpster of some apartment complex. I didn't want whatever was in the nice gift bag anywhere near my apartment.

"Damn. I thought y'all were perfect for each other," Mya says. "Yea, well I guess we weren't the perfect match," I say.

"Don't trip thought," Mya says. "You young and you still look good. Somebody will scoop you and the kids up with no problem."

I love Mya to death. She knows people fuck with me because of how I look, but she doesn't care. She knows that rolling with me could lead to people posting pictures with my eyebrows on her face, but she remains loyal.

I'm not gone lie. Matt not calling me back hurt like hell. Especially when I figured out why. But I know there's a husband out there for me. I have two baby daddies, so I know I can get a man. But now that there's a little fame following me, it's about finding a man that can deal with the downside of it.

I don't pity myself. I just hate how many fucked up and heartless people roam the earth. There's too many people that don't care about anyone's feelings but their own.

I leave to pick up the boys. My heart drops and my stomach turns when I see fire fighters and police cars. The only good things is I don't see a fire. I park illegally on the wrong side of the street, search for my boys and call them at the same time.

"Where are you?" I ask.

I'm relieved at the sound of Justin's voice. I'm catching my breath.

"Upstairs," Justin says.

"I'm outside," I say. "What happened?"

"Someone pulled the fire alarm," Justin says.

"Is everyone okay?" I ask.

Justin says yes.

When I get upstairs it seems the party ended a little earlier because all I see are Grace, Justin, Josiah and some other girl I do not know.

"Where's your parents?" I ask Grace.

"They ran downstairs," Grace says.

Grace looks like she's lying and the boys look like they been up to no good.

"They just went down like ten seconds before you knocked," Grace says. "I'm surprised you didn't see them."

"Okay, well tell them I said bye," I say. "Happy birthday."

My minds got a lot running through it right now.

"Josiah who was that other lil' girl in the room with y'all?" I ask.

"One of Grace's friends," Josiah says.

"When were you going to call and tell me the party ended and a fire might've broke out?" I ask.

"There wasn't a fire," Josiah's smart self says.

"You didn't know off the top of your head to call and tell me there might have been one?" I ask.

54

I'm fussing.

I'm just pure mad.

I know Grace was lying about how long they were alone, and I think the gold digging Wallace's left them on purpose. They're prepping their daughter for the eighteen year check at thirteen years old.

"Forget about that high school party next weekend," I say.

The boys are pissed.

Chapter 17

One of Alisa's teammates is having a party for the dance team. KI stay the whole time. My lil' girl at a high school party just not gone fly. I can see the entire backyard from where I'm sitting in the dining room.

Alisa and her team mainly discuss what goes on at school, dance, look at pictures of themselves, and enjoy the food.

Afterwards, me and Alisa hold hands and walk around Hollywood. She's just like her mother. She loves to be out and about late at night. We're night people.

I can't wait until my kids are eighteen or sixteen at that. Once they can drive it's on and poppin'. We gone be out enjoying the night life all the time.

I take the boys off restrictions when I get home and they apologize and say they love me. They repeatedly kiss me on the cheek.

"Y'all better stop doing all this kissing on me," I say. "People gone start thinking y'all want y'all momma if they don't already."

"Mom, people gone always think that because you look the same age as us," Justin says.

Little does he know he just described his girl.

I go to bed and my sleep is interrupted by, "Stop talking Bianca!" Stacey's yelling at her because she's trying to sleep.

"Be quiet over there!" Charise yells across the hall.

I turn the light on in Bianca and Stacey's room. Bianca's making conversation with her dolls.

"Put that up," I say to Bianca. "It's bedtime. This is the last time I want to get woke up by anybody in this house. When I'm in my room sleep that means keep it down."

I shut the light off. I hate dealing with this pettiness. But I'd rather deal with this than Stacey peeing in the bed. She just broke the habit not too long ago. It's not that she can't get out the

bed, it's that she's too lazy. Pretty much she didn't feel like walking to the bathroom and breaking her dream so she would just say fuck it and wake up wet.

I started taking Stacey's toys away and making her stay in the room all day. It got the job done. She hasn't been pissy for a while.

Grace puts in overtime to show Justin that she loves his mother. She sits in between my legs at every game on the row in front of me. She always holds my hand. She ever volunteers to go to the concessions for me.

Takes me a few games, but I catch onto what she's really doing when a few girls walk past us. She's letting them know that she already has one of the boys to herself. She's also letting them know she's already in good with the family, which means she's been around for a minute. I can't take it with this girl. I'm sure her parents coached her on how to act. She's lucky I like her and I'm over what she said.

Grace's sister brings her by the house I allow it this one time. I can't hall all sever of my kids friends popping up.

Chapter 18

The boys win the state tournament by fifty-two points. It felt like a professional basketball game due to all the celebrities and athletes that showed up to watch.

The boys are getting interviewed backstage.

Me and the girls are so happy for them.

"I'm so proud of you," I tell Alisa.

She did great during the half time show.

Chapter 19

The boys have what is their last team dinner at Coach Eric's house and that's that.

Finally free from basketball.

"Congratulations on a great season boys," I tell my boys' team when I pick them up.

I thank Coach Eric for allowing them to play and he says no problem.

"You guys going to miss your teammates?" I ask Justin and Josiah in the car.

"No," Josiah says.

"If we see them around, we see them around," Justin says. "If not, they still have each other."

Chapter 20

I call a family meeting and say exactly what it is right now.

"For the next two weeks we're not doing or going anywhere," I say. "We're about to be best friends with this house. I'm tired. I'm really tired okay. After these two weeks, I will homeschool you guys alright. But for now. I need a break."

"Can you pull us out now Mom please?" Justin begs. "We can teach ourselves and we can help with the girls."

"You guys don't want to spend more time with your friends at school?" I ask.

"No," they all say in unison.

"Why?" I ask.

"We have their phone numbers Mom," Justin says. "Please pull us out. I'm already tired of sitting in class all day. I'm a fast learner."

"Fine. I'll pull you guys out and you better do the work and not slack off," I say.

The kids do schoolwork during the day and record songs at night. While they're focusing on school work, I write scripts for their shows.

Bianca and Stacey's show will center around them at school. Bianca's character will be misbehaved. Her mother will constantly receive phone calls from the school to pick her up and Stacey's character will be a good one. The show will be about the mother trying to figure out why one of her daughters is a problem child. It will be because one of the older kids at the school always picks on her and tells her if she snitches the whole school will make fun of her.

Lanice and Charise's show will be about their journey leading their dance team to nationals.

Justin, Josiah, and Alisa's show will be about two brothers trying to help their sister recover from being sexually assaulted. Alisa's character, who is the victim, will keep making attempts at

killing herself. The kids are already in the care of their auntie because their mother passed and their sister is the only person they have that reminds them of her.

We record on the weekends.

Chapter 21

For Bianca's birthday we go to Pizza Palace, where the kids have fun in a big castle that has playground things inside.

Days later, I surprise Bianca and Stacey by setting up an audition for a kid's talent show. First prize is fifty thousand dollars.

The kids wait on the side of the stage while I tell the stage manager how the lighting and effects should be for the girls.

"Josiah or Justin, one of y'all warm them up please," I say.

The DJ plays a nice hip hop instrumental and Bianca and Stacey follow Josiah's lead with stretches and the dances they do to warm-up.

When Bianca and Stacey audition, they don't mess up at all. They really just did that. I mean they completely showed out.

the judges, Natalia, Niecy, and Porter, and producers of the show are stunned. Bianca and Stacey are given microphones.

"That was absolutely amazing," Natalia says. "Did you two learn that on your own?"

"We went to the dance studio and my brother helped us too," Bianca says.

"What is you girls biggest dream in life?" Natalia asks. "Do you want to be singers and dancers?"

"Yes," Stacey says. "Our biggest dream is to put on a show at Star Lanes Center."

"I bet you can make that happen," Natalia says. "Now I know you girls come from a family of many. How many brothers and sisters do you have?"

Here we go.

"Two brothers and three more sisters," Bianca says.

They're doing a good job of alternating responses like we talked about.

The judges ask for me and the rest of my kids to come out.

"Now who is the mother?" Porter asks.

Stacey gives me a hug.

"I'm just kidding," Porter says. "I'm a fan of your brothers. I was honored to catch one of their games."

"Let me just say this," Niecy says. "You look absolutely amazing. You have seven kids and you look better than most people that only have one."

I'm just waiting to hear Bianca and Stacey made it to the next round.

"Well I tell you what," Niecy continues. "You girls are going to the next round."

Bianca and Stacey end up winning the entire competition.

After they get their first place trophies, me and all of my kids hang out on stage. The girls are enjoying playing with the balloons that fell from the ceiling. Justin is playing around, singing, with the microphone that's not on. Someone in the audience wants to hear his voice so someone cuts it on. Justin gets nervous and stops.

"Can we hear you sing?" Porter asks.

Justin sings and the judge is amazed. Now he wants to hear all my kids sing. He can't believe their talent. His face says it all. He'll be contacting me sometime soon to sign some contracts.

While we're hopping in the car outside, some annoying and clearly bitter black man says, "She got seven kids. But not nobody wife her. She got seven kids."

Anyways. To celebrate Bianca and Stacey's win, we go out to dinner and play games all night at the house.

Josiah starts imitating Bianca and Stacey's dance moves.

"show me how to do that dance you did," Josiah tells Stacey.

She teaches him and me and the rest of the clan learn it too.

We eat junk food until our bellies are about to explode, then call it a night.

The kids sleep great.

I don't.

I should've stayed off the blogs. People think I have more

than two baby daddies. On top of that I got my stupid middle and high school flings posting on social media that the kids are potentially theirs.

To make matters worse, Stacey and Bianca's dad is lying saying I'm keeping the kids from him. He just wants attention and to stop paying child support.

I don't have time for this. I don't have any reason to clarify anything to people don't know.

Let me make something clear about my relations hip with the blogs: I don't read them for gossip on other celebrities. I read them to see what people are saying about me. I like to know what people are saying about me and how they're looking at me. If they are disturbed about something about me, then if I ever see them, I will gladly walk the other way or make it known with my eyes that I don't want them talking to me.

Chapter 22

The kids and I attend a picnic at a park for an author I met at one of my seminars. Her name is Teresa. She's very successful and I was honored she thought enough of me to come hear me speak.

"Congratulations," I say hugging Teresa. Stacey gives her a hug too. I love her little self. She always wants to make someone fell special and loved.

"This is my friend Mya," I say to Teresa.

"Hello," Teresa says. "Leah your kids are so cute."

I say thank you. The boys give Teresa a hug.

"They gone be some heartbreakers," Teresa says.

Josiah shakes his head with the biggest smile on his face. They love hearing they look good from other people.

Grace is here.

I know my kids wouldn't invite someone to a function I was invited to.

Seriously.

"How did she know we were here?" I ask.

Grace gives Justin a hug.

"I take it that's his girlfriend," Teresa says.

"Friend," I say.

I know it's his girlfriend and I call her that sometimes. I just don't want the world thinking I'm okay with this relationship stuff this young.

Me, Teresa and Mya walk around the park for a while.

Then me and Mya watch the kids enjoy themselves on the playground.

"So me and Mya going out tonight," I say to my kids. "Who gone watch y'all?"

"Mommy it's my turn," Alisa says. "Evan came over here last time."

Alisa's teammate Marissa comes by. I give her the same speech I gave Evan. The kids can do everything on their own.

She's just here for supervision in case for some reason someone shows up and needs to speak to an adult.

"Ms. Leah, when can I go out with y'all?" Marissa asks. She's watching me and Mya put our makeup on.

"I'm eighteen," Marissa continues. "I'm trying to be on with y'all."

"Girl. When you can drink, you can roll with us," I say.

"I can get a fake I.D.," Marissa says.

Me and Mya are cracking up. Pretty much letting this girl know we're not taking any risk on her getting caught sneaking in any place and on top of that, buying her alcohol. We're the ones that's gone get hit with some type of consequences for distributing to a minor if she start acting a fool in public.

Chapter 23

Mya and I attend my release party for my book <u>Divorce</u> at a lounge. <u>Divorce</u> is simply about a couple that divorced and their kids do deceitful things to get them back together.

Friends, drinks and conversation is all I needed.

When I get back to the house, Marissa and Alisa are sleep in the den. I can bet money Alisa told Charise and Lanice to find something to do in another part of the house. She probably wants a feel of having an older sister too.

"So how was it spending time with Marissa?" I ask. Alisa the next morning. She says fine. Then I ask Justin, "How did Grace know we would be at that park?"

"I don't know," Justin says.

"You didn't say anything to her about it?" I ask.

"I told her we were going but I didn't tell her she could come," Justin says. "I said it was for one of your friends. I thought she knew it was common courtesy to not just show up. Especially when the party wasn't for me."

"Son, is this girl obsessed with you?" I ask.

Justin looks down at the floor.

Anyways.

Now it's time for me to devote time into Alisa, Lanice and Charise.

I enter the girls in a dance competition. I wish I would've done my research on it first because I do not like these grown dance moves I've been watching them practice. I also don't like these leotards they chose to wear, but I don't want them to feel like outcast at the competition.

Me, Josiah, Justin, Bianca and Stacey can't believe our eyes the day of the competition. Watching these kids compete is way too much for us.

There's a group of five year olds in skirts shaking they little behinds side to side. One of their parents on the front row keeps

saying, "shake that booty." He sounds foul as hell.

My girls take the stage and the crowd goes crazy before they even move. Kids are already chanting their names. The music comes on and all I see is ass shaking, flips, splits, and a bunch of other seductive moves. Some of the routine is appropriate, but most of it's not.

They will not be participating in this again.

Chapter 24

Me and the kids spend the day checking out Mya's new one bedroom apartment. I don't know how I should feel about two ambulance trucks being parked across the street on my first visit.

"I'm so happy for you girl," I say to Mya as we chill in her living room.

"It feels good," Mya says.

"You feel like a brand new person huh?" I ask. "Believe me I know the feeling."

"Ms. Mya you should have a house warming party," Josiah suggests.

"Nope," Mya says. "When you've lived my life you don't want to have social gatherings even if they are a bunch of people you've known for a while."

"Why?" Stacey asks.

"Excuse me," I say. "That's not your business."

"Naw, it's cool," Mya says. "People stole from my family a lot growing up. Someone stole my mom's car keys one time and drove off with her car. Police never found him. Or her. People are thieves. You got to keep your eyes and ears opened. I'm cool being in my new spot with no one knowing where I live except my mom and you guys."

Me, Mya and the kids spend an hour in the workout room before grilling burgers and chicken by the pool. Some sixteen year old boy asks for my number.

"Lil' boy I'm grown," I say.

When I turn around Mya is laughing.

"Girl don't trip," Mya says. "When you forty years old, people still gone be trying to get with you."

Chapter 25

I call Mya the next morning to bring Alisa's purse she left at her apartment, and hear sirens.

What's going on?" I ask.

"Girl the ambulance is across the street again," Mya says.

"For what?" I ask.

"I think it's some elderly people they keep coming for," Mya says.

"Every day?" I ask.

"I don't know," Mya says. "But I'm on my way to you. I'm in need of a new atmosphere."

The next day I get an email inviting my kids to the red carpet for a singer that calls himself Blade.

It's tonight. Blade's agent invited them. I take the girls to pick out some cute dresses, the boys get nice outfits, and we attend. They absolutely love even more that people are interviewing them.

I'm in the background taking everything in. I let the kids wander off together until I see this old man taking a little too much interest in them. Especially Alisa. He's given her multiple hugs and kisses on the cheek. He keeps rubbing her back. His face is lit completely up. He just can't stop touching her. It's irking me.

I walk over and introduce myself.

"Hi, I'm Leah. The girl's mom," I say.

"Nice to meet you in person. Thanks for accepting my invitation." It's Blade's agent. Go figure. "You're daughters are very lovely."

"Thanks," my girls say.

"Here's my card," Blades agent says. "I'm sure with the right help they can go extremely far."

As soon as I get home I'm throwing it away.

Aside from that strange man, I'm enjoying the red carpet.

It's not until Vayda makes it her business to walk in front of me that I lose my want to be here. I don't want to, but my eyes devilishly follow her. She walks right up to Terry Black, a pop singer that loves to post pictures talking bad about my eyebrows. What are the odds they're both here. I can't wait to leave.

On the way out, Terry makes it his business to find me.

"Hey I wanted to apologize for what I did," Terry says.

Unfortunately he's a great actor and I have no way of knowing he's sincere.

"Sometimes the kid in me comes out," Terry continues.

He's really serious right now. He thinks I'm buying his stupid apology.

I still say, "Don't worry about it."

Terry wasn't going to leave unless I said something. He gives me an air kiss on the cheek then finally moves out my way. As soon as he does, there Vayda is. She's waving hi to me with a huge smile on her face. I say hi back. She kisses my cheek.

So this is what I have to take a chance on every time I go to these events. Seeing all these fake ass people that know I won't act an ass or bring up old stuff at such a class event.

Chapter 26

Summer is finally here and I couldn't be happier until I get a call from Coach Eric. He wants the boys to play on hi summer team.

I talk to the boys about it in their rooms.

"We can be titled the best point guards in the country if we make it to nationals Mom," Josiah says.

I take that as a yes they want to play.

"Alright. I'll call Coach and let him know you guys are on board," I say.

Justin and Josiah get off their beds, hug me tight, tackle me to the floor and kiss my cheeks.

"We love you Momma," Justin says.

I don't respond so they tickle me.

"Huh?" Josiah says. "We can't hear you."

I'm laughing too hard. I'm trying to get what I want to say out but can't.

"Pick her up and throw her on the bed," Josiah says.

He grabs my legs and Justin grabs my arms and they swing me back and forth prepping to toss me.

"Y'all bet not throw me on this bed," I say.

"We can't hear you," Justin says.

"I said I love you," I say.

"Who's you?" Justin asks.

"The both of you," I say.

"We love you too Mom," Josiah says.

The boys toss me on the bed and run out the room. I run after them but can't find them.

They're hiding.

I go in Alisa's room and the girls have pillows tucked under their sheets.

Charise jumps on my back from behind.

"Where are the boys at?" I ask.

"I don't know," Charise laughs.

Bianca and Stacey are peaking in Alisa's room.

They lead me to the backyard.

Soon as I step out the screen door, the boys scare me and start shooting me with their toy guns.

"Here Mommy," Stacey says.

She hands me a weapon.

The whole house is playing *War.*

I'm tired after only a couple minutes.

I fall on the couch.

Me and the girls cuddle together and watch a show called *Evil Encounters* in the den.

"That was fun Mommy," Stacey says.

I can't even bring myself to speak I'm so out of breath.

The show goes on a commercial and I flip through the channels. I stop when I hear my name. Me and the kids tune into the reporter with a picture of me next to pop singer Terry Black and his girlfriend Kristina Thorn on the screen.

"Is Terry Black and his girlfriend feuding with Leah Rogers?" the reporter asks. "People are speculating this because last night Black posted this photo of the author on his page."

A picture of me next to a girl with thin pretty eyebrows.

"Thorn reposted the photo to her twenty-two million followers," the reporter says. "Both later deleted the photos and said they were just fooling around. They didn't mean any harm. No word or posting from Rogers on the incident."

The reporter switches subjects and I turn back to *Evil Encounters.*

Here I am, once again, embarrassed in front of my kids. I can't stand a lot of these immature celebrities. They know exactly what they're doing when they post stuff to their millions of fans then delete it. They're not stupid. It's not anyone's fault that people pick them apart every day. It's definitely not mine.

Terry and Kristina doing that to me for no reason is just pure evil. I'm sure they just wanted to read comments or take the

attention off of their abusive relationship for a while. Perhaps sit around and post and read negative stuff about them all the time, so they probably feel it's only right to do the same thing to me.

I can't stand these heartless gossip stations either. They don't have to add to this mess by broadcasting to even more people the pictures.

My kids look so fed up with people ridiculing me. I know they're hurting too because Terry is one of their favorite signers and Kristina is one of their favorite beauties. They joy they had in them before I turned to the news just vanished. They're not even interested in the show anymore.

To try and cheer my kids up, I shoot music videos with them and their friends at various locations. I shoot one video each for all of them, and post them on a website I created. In less than a week they all have millions of views. I'm glad I went with my instincts and let ads post on my page to generate some revenue.

My book sales are slowing down and I need this income right now.

I create another site to release videos of their web shows.

As their video views go up, so does the crowds at the basketball games. Everyone doesn't even get to watch the game sometimes because the gym is so packed.

After two games the staff at the gyms have to do crowd control the entire game. Girls are running on the cour after my boys. Someone has to stand in front of each section to make sure no one runs on the court.

After practices and games, there are people waiting to snap pictures of all of my kids.

Chapter 27

Everyone spends their time practicing their songs.

Our next stop is performing at a few places once the boys finish with basketball. I spend a few hours a day teaching Bianca and Stacey how to read. If they want to act and sing they will have to learn because Mommy doesn't want to keep drilling the words in their brain then have to rehearse with them. That's too much. They either learn to read or they'll just be dancing.

All me and the kids do is work, eat and sleep. We don't have a single issue until Alisa, Charise and Lanice start wondering why they haven't gotten any money off their videos or web shows.

"Do you guys think this house, food and the clothes you wear are free?" I ask furiously. I'm about to go off. "I bought those cameras, paid professionals to shoot the videos, paid for producers, spent hours editing the footage, paid for the extras. On top of that, I wrote the shows."

They all look stupid.

"I haven't wrote a book in a while," I say. "And who can tell me why? No one wants to answer now huh? If you three want, I can cut out your activities and spend that time writing. That way Mommy can make more of her own money."

"We're sorry Mom," Alisa says. "We weren't thinking about all that."

"I suggest you guys go to your room before I delete what I put up and focus on what I want to do in place of what you want to do," I say.

They have some nerve coming at me with that mess. They're lucky I love them.

Chapter 28

I get invited to a house party by this famous actor named Robert Young. He's this fine looking man with six number one films under his belt. I look at all his pages to see who he has pictures with. Yes! None with Vayda. None with Terry and Kristina. And none with any of the other heartless people I can't stand looking at.

I type Robert's name in the search bar with mine just to be sure he hasn't posted or said anything foul about me. There's nothing.

I want to invite Mya to the party, but I need her to watch the kids, so I'm riding solo.

Robert greets me with a hug as soon as I get out the car. He wants to collaborate on a book so I brought my laptop. I'm leaving it in the car for now though.

"How are you?" Robert asks.

He's really happy I came.

"Good," I say. "Thanks for inviting me."

We go to the backyard. He has a table full of food that his guests are enjoying and music playing.

"How are you and the kids?" Robert asks.

"We're good," I say. "Busier than I'd like to be, but we're good."

"Be sure to tell your boys I said congratulations," Robert says.

He introduces me to his sister and a few of his cousins, then we make ourselves a plate. I chat with a few people.

The atmosphere gives me the vibe of a family reunion. Everyone's catching up about something, sharing hugs and kisses and enjoying each other's company.

Unfortunately the rain kills the flow. Some people go inside, but mostly everyone leaves. I would've left to if I'd have known Vayda was inside with her crew. I can't even hide that I'm

disgusted to see her yet again.

"Hi Leah," Vayda says.

"Hi," I say without looking at her and take a seat on the couch in front of her.

In about ten minutes I'm gone have one of my kids call me so I can get out of here. There's no way I'm staying here.

"I really love her books," Vayda says to some lady sitting next to her.

She wants everyone to hear her speak well of me.

"I wish she didn't hate me," Vayda says.

I'm not paying her no mind not looking at her.

"Leah can you sign my book?" Vayda asks.

This is one annoying girl. She knows just how to force someone into a position they don't want to be in. I don't want to sign it. I don't want to be close to her, but I'll look like the bitch if I don't' right? She did support my sales. I kneel down next to her, sign it and take my seat.

Now she's making conversation with her so-called friend Kalia. They're learning about each other's projects. These girls are pathetic. From what I read online thye don't even like each other. However they do have something in common: they're both dumb as all hell. They're those dumb people that think they're so smart. They think they're the ones with the brains an everyone else is the idiots. I'll admit I have a bad habit of enjoying reading negative stories about people I don't like. Don't judge me. I'm working on myself.

But anyways, it was rumored that Kalia slept with Vayda's baby daddy so he could put her in his film. Kalia never denied it. The following week the top gossip website's headline post was:

Vayda is pregnant by Kalia's baby daddy.

Vayda instantly hopped online and denied it. What was interesting about her denying it was she never denied the countless other people that she was rumored to be pregnant by.

But she took this one personal. Everyone knows Vayda and Kalia slept with each other's men. Any idiot could put those big ass pieces together. One thing I don't like about Kalia and Vayda is that they are both known home-wreckers.

This entertainment industry is so fake. I think girls that try to get back at one another by sleeping with each other's boyfriends, exes, baby daddies, or husbands are so trifling. I mean that about the men too. However, I think some men just couldn't be happier they have another cut buddy.

Kalia and Vayda are both pathetic and everyone in the industry knows it. There was a rumor that when they were both on the brink of stardom they already had a list of celebrities that they had on their *to sleep with* list.

Back to the party though.

Most of the people in the room are having side conversations. I'm about to press send on this message to my son, but Robert interrupts me.

"You want to start working on the story Leah?" Robert asks.

I get my computer out the car. On my way back in, some people are on their way out. Vayda and her crew are the only ones still here.

I couldn't leave right now if I wanted to. Someone's car is blocking mine.

Oh well. I meet Robert in his office room like he asked. Of course he's not in it. I set up my computer and get comfortable. I have to be completely at ease when I work on my craft.

Five minutes passes and Robert still hasn't came in. I peak my head out the door and there's no sight of him. To make matters worse, I got to use the bathroom now.

Takes me a good three minutes to find a door that leads to a toilet in Robert's big mansion. After I release myself, I don't want to leave the bathroom. This is the most spacious bathroom I've ever been in. I want to hop in his shower. I slide a mirror door over and it leads to a huge closet. I'm looking at my shape

in his mirror.

I'm trying to do as much as I can in here.

I lean against the wall and picture me and Westin making love in his bathroom. On the counter, in the closet and in the shower. We would tear some stuff up in here.

To be honest, if I didn't have all these kids I would already be living like this. Taking care of them and putting time into the things they want to do sets me all the way back.

But, like I said, I wouldn't trade them for the world.

I go back in the office and ...

Wait a minute.

My computer and phone are not in here. I'm looking high and low for my phone. I know someone moved my computer. Shit. I don't know why I would leave anything in here if I knew people were still here.

I find Robert in the backyard cleaning up now that the rain has stopped.

"Do you know where those girls went?" I angrily ask.

"What girls?" Robert asks.

"Vayda and her crew," I say.

"Chill," Robert says. "Wasup?"

"They took my computer and my phone," I say.

"Relax," Robert says.

"Relax? I have a lot of important stuff on both of them," I say.

Oh no. My phone doesn't have a password. I'm crying.

Robert's calling someone. He got sent to voicemail. I follow him inside. We're looking in the rooms. No ones in the first few.

We reach a room that's locked.

"Open the door whoever's in here!" Robert yells.

No one says anything.

Robert's friend Marshell walks up behind us and says she's leaving. I didn't know anyone else besides Vayda and her crew was still here.

"Leah are you okay?" Marshell asks.

I lean against the wall, slide down to the floor and cover my face. Marshell kneels down in front of me.

"Vayda and her peoples have my computer and phone," I say. "I don't know what they're doing with them."

"Did you see them come in here?" Robert asks Marshell.

"I saw them walk upstairs but I don't know if they all went in here," Marshell answers. "I'm trying to leave but your car is blocking me," she says to Robert.

"Someone's blocking me in too," I say.

"What the fuck is going on? Why are they doing this to her?" Marshell asks Robert.

"Girls can you please give Leah her things back?" Robert asks. "We got shit to do."

They don't say anything.

"Look, I'm going to let her out then I'll be right back," Robert whispers to me. Him and Marshell get all the way down the steps, then Marshell stops and shows Robert something on her phone.

"Leah did you do anything to them?" Marshell asks me.

"Not that I know of," I bitterly say. "Why?"

Marshell shows me her phone. All my posts on *FriendSpot* and *ChitChatFam* have been deleted and replaced with disrespectful pictures that people created of me. There's all types of lies planted on my page calling me a tramp and saying I slept with a bunch of celebrities. There's even lies saying I regret my kids and I hired a ghost writer to write all my books.

"Can I use your computer?" I ask Marshell.

I need to delete this shit and let everyone know what's going on.

Unfortunately I can't. Vayda and her crew changed all my passwords.

Roberts beating on the door now.

"This shit not funny," Robert says. "Come on. We need to talk about whatever the fuck is going on."

80

The thieves in the room still don't say nothing.

"You want a ride home?" Marshell asks me.

"No. I want to call the police," I say.

"Look," Robert says. "I don't want to be on the news tomorrow for this. Please. Let me pay you. I'll give you anything you and your kids want. But please don't make a scene at my house."

I'm not gone get the authorities involved. Which is fucked up because once I leave I have no proof they took my shit. They're the only ones here right now. If they stay in this room I would be good. But the bigger picture is that all the lies that have been posted can't be undone. And when I say undone, I mean erased out of everyone's memory. Sure me clearing it up will put me back in good standing with a lot of people, but not with all people. There's always those people that believe everything they read.

"Come with me," Marshell says. "There's plenty of ways you can let everybody know what happened tomorrow or when you get home tonight. Just go home and sleep this off."

I follow Marshell outside. We got to our cars. When she pulls off I remember I left my plate in the fridge.

I hear noises in the other room.

I peak my head in and Vayda and one of her girls are giving Robert head.

Fuck this lying ass bastard Robert.

My computer and phone are nowhere in sight. They must've hid them.

"Marshell can I use your phone again?" I ask.

I call the police. A squad car arrives immediately. I tell them what happened and they take the report outside. Robert is furious. So is Vayda and her girls.

Marshell is back.

"Can you search his house?" I ask the police.

"They're not searching anything without a warrant," Robert

angrily says.

The officers advise me to let the public know my account was hacked and to move on.

"There's a lot of people that have worse stories out there than you," one of the officers says.

"I don't know what the fuck is up with those girls," I tell Marshell.

"Have you ever said anything about them in the past, slept with someone they know, girl what?" Marshell asks. "They just fuckin' wit you to fuck with you?"

"I honestly can't think of shit I've done to any of them," I say. "Now I got to go home, create another account and explain to everyone what happened."

"I know you don't want to hear this, but I don't think you should say names," Marshell says.

She's a damn fool.

"Why not?" I ask.

"Because for one, you know they gone deny it," Marshell says. "It's just gone be more mess. Your kids got a lot going on for them and you don't want to overshadow it feuding with them bitches. And you know I don't got no reason to care for any of they asses. I know you're smart and can catch vibes. You know me and that bitch Vayda don't like each other. Just tell everyone your computer and phone were stolen and move on. Karma will catch those bitches."

Chapter 29

"Mommy someone hacked your account," Charise says when I get home.

"Girl what's going on?" Mya asks concerned. "I'm getting all types of shit from your phone. The kids are too. Your accounts got all types of bullshit on them. It's broadcasting all over gossip shows."

I look through my messages sent to Mya's phone.

Die. You need help. So damn stupid. Off with your head.

I'm angry as all hell.

"And where is your car?" Mya asks looking outside.

People fucking with me, and I don't have a clue what for, is driving me up the damn wall. I cry to my kids and ask them to hop online and tell everyone my stuff was stolen. I don't tell them who took it. They don't need to know.

"I already did Mom," Alisa says. " I knew you wouldn't do anything like that."

"Alisa, what kinds of messages were they sending you guys?" I ask.

"I don't remember," Alisa says. "I already deleted them. Don't worry about it Mom. It's okay."

"You guys go to bed so I can talk to Mya for a minute," I say. "Josiah pour me two glasses of wine please before you do."

I down my first glass and shut the door.

"It's that bitch Vayda," I say to Mya.

"What," Mya says. "She don't know about the video does she?"

"No," I say. "I don't even have it no more. It's nowhere on the internet either. I probably didn't even save it or accidently deleted it or something."

"Wow. So that bitch really went in all your shit and posted that stuff," Mya says. "She needs her ass beat."

83

I know," I say. "But you already know I got to look out for my kids."

I can't risk spending nights in jail and my kids getting taken away because they're not old enough to stay home alone.

"I know," Mya says. "Let me put on my account too that your shit got stolen."

"Thanks girl," I say.

I tell her not to put names.

"You want me to stay or you alright?" Mya asks.

"I'm alright," I say.

I stay up walking around my room and refilling my glasses of wine all night. I'm thinking of revenge that's worth my while and won't get me locked up if it's traced back to me, but can't come up with anything. I can't let Vayda and her crew break me. I know they're waiting for me to hop online and expose they asses just so they can deny it and laugh all night.

I hate these messy ass industry bitches.

I get a new phone the next day. Of course I make sure to put a passcode on it. I call the companies for my accounts that have been hacked and have them terminated.

I buy two new computers.

One will never leave the house. That will be the one that has all my writings on it.

Chapter 30

The boys need this game to advance to the championship. I'm sure everyone else just like myself isn't worried about anything. I feel like the trophy should just be given to us right now.

Everyone thinks their team will be the one to beat us and they always get their feelings hurt. They come up with what they think are good game plans and my boys demolish them horribly.

We win the game by sixty.

When I get home I have an email from Terry Black's manager. He wants me to dance in Terry's next video. I'm contemplating. Yes I could use the money, but at the same time I don't want that heartless bastard thinking he can do what he wants as long as he gives me an opportunity to put myself out there more. Which I don't even care to do.

All of a sudden he wants to work together. I know it's because my boys are getting ga lot of recognition.

The only reason that I'm actually thinking about giving it a shot is because we could become cool then my kids wouldn't have to pretend not to like him to me and the rest of the world.

They could meet one of their favorite people, take pictures with him and be happy. Who knows. They could probably end up being friends.

Forget that. None of it should matter. It shouldn't be about being in the company of talented people just because they have a gift. Forget about Terry knowing how to sing, act and dance, and on top of that being a gold medalist in the Olympics.

The heart is what should count first.

I'm not doing not one single project with him. He created several pictures. Then he had to save it to his computer. He still didn't have second thoughts. He had to upload it to his account. That didn't stop him. Then he had to click post.

Terry wanted to be a jackass. And for that reason, I hope I never have to see him again.

If I liked him I wouldn't mind working with him and getting a little publicity because he does have a huge fan base. But I don't want anything for the wrong reasons.

Plus, my discernment is telling me he did what he did to make people laugh. He knew he would apologize and invite me to be in his video before he even posted that last photo of me.

It was all planned.

We will be enemies forever.

Chapter 31

I can't sleep. Not because I'm angry about something but because I'm happy. My sons were so proud talking about me to their friends. I heard them talking about me on their phones.

I feel so accomplished in raising my children. I'm about to go check on my babies.

Okay. So Alisa, Charise and Lanice are not in their room and neither is Bianca and Stacey. I don't know what's going on, but before I scream let me check the boy's room. The door is shut but I hear laughing. I almost grip the doorknob, but I hear Charise's voice.

"She needs to dress better and stop embarrassing us," Charise says.

The rest of my kids are laughing. Bianca and Stacey are laughing the loudest.

I've never heard them laugh like this before. It's coming from deep within.

"The way she dresses isn't up to date," Charise says. "Does anyone here even like the clothes she picks out for us?"

No one says anything. They're just laughing.

"I'm embarrassed enough that people keep staring at her weird," Charise says. "Thank goodness we didn't get those eyebrows. I can't stand sitting next to her when people do that. It's just fucking embarrassing."

Tears are falling down my face. My heart is burning. I never heard Charise curse. I never heard any of my kids use foul language and the first time I do it's because of how I was born.

They're embarrassed by me.

I'm doing everything I can to not make any sounds. I want to hear what else my daughter thinks of me.

"She's always saying dumb stuff too," Lanice says.

"What grown woman would make an email account Leah-four-five Williams?" Charise asks.

The laughter erupts in the room.

"Keep it down," Alisa warns them. "We don't want to wake her up."

They get louder.

"Do it again," Josiah says.

I don't know who he's talking to. I guess someone is acting something out. Whoever he's talking to must've done it because they're laughing again. I think it's Bianca because I don't hear her loud voice.

"And that is why you are my favorite sister," Josiah says.

It was Bianca.

"I fuckin' can't stand Mom." Charise is back at it.

She's doing the most talking.

"A few months ago I snuck in her room and deleted this video of Vayda Mom showed me," Charise says.

This little bitch. I'm furious now. I want to break down this door but I want to hear more.

"What video?" Alisa asks.

"She had footage of Vayda hitting and dragging her son in the hotel lobby," Charise says. "She hit him on his head real hard too. I knew she would release it one day to get back at her but I wasn't gone let that happen."

"I'm surprised she didn't wake up," Josiah says.

"Please. I went in her room like a little mouse," Charise laughs. "Vayda is so beautiful. I wish she was our mom."

I'm crying harder now. My tears are so thick I'm surprised they can't hear them hit the floor.

"I mean just imagine what could happen if our mom was a world class beauty," Charise says.

"I feel you on that," Alisa says. "Sometimes I have to photoshop, crop, just pure transform me and mom's pictures just so her eyebrows don't look so off."

"That shit gets annoying," Justin says.

"I want her to have someone fix her eyebrows," Charise says.

Those words hit my heart like fire. No one has ever opened their mouths to tell me I should get my eyebrows fixed.

I can't believe what I'm hearing these kids say. I'm starting to question if I'm being selfish by not getting my eyebrows changed.

I should have known my kids would hate dealing with a mother that attracts the wrong attention. I'm so hurt right now I can't believe I'm still standing and breathing. My heart is torn listening to what my kids that I chose to keep when I got pregnant, talk about me. If I would've known they would rip me apart like this I wouldn't have had them. They don't even sound like my kids anymore. They sound like some grown ass adults having a conversation about some bitch they can't stand. These aren't my sweet innocent kids.

It gets quiet for a second then Justin says, "I get tired of not being able to speak to my favorite celebrities because I'll look stupid because I'm smiling with people that talk bad about her. I hate it."

"I'm just so sick of it," Charise says.

Now she's laughing.

"What?" Josiah asks.

"Mom still has that notice from Maxine's company on her page," Charise says.

Maxine is a famous actress. She was shopping in the store one day and I ran into her. I asked her for a picture and she happily said yes. I posted it on my account and tagged her. Next thing I knew I had a notice saying it was deleted by her company.

Back then I was naïve. I had no clue why they took it down. When I got older, I realized the ugly truth. From the angle the photo was taken, my eyebrows looked terrible. Maxine knew the evil people in the world would make jokes about the photo so she had it removed.

I never took down the deletion notice because I was

determined to be someone one day and I wanted that bitch to live with regret for the rest of her life.

Maxine had her fucking company take down all the pictures from the internet and when my first book was released, which she says is her favorite book, she started sending the photo we took together around to blog sites. She even got in contact with me. She wanted to do lunch. I hung up in her face.

Fuck her and everyone else that gives me a hard time.

"Hey, you better delete that page before she find out it's you that created that shit," Justin says.

"She not gone find out," Charise says. "I will keep updating this account. I like to read the comments. I delete all the ones defending her. Those aren't fun. But anyways, I hit up somebody that Vayda was following so she could know that I saved her from."

"Who is he?" Justin says.

He sounds annoyed.

"Relax brother," Charise says. "He's just her cousin or something and the same age as me. I got his number too. Vayda got on the phone and said hi to me one day."

I'm still crying. But my tears slowly stop when I come to a realization of how I'm gone get back at these disrespectful, fake ass kids.

Shit. Somebody about to walk out the room. I walk briskly back upstairs.

I'm in my bed pissed thee fuck off. I can't believe they asses. I'm good as fuck to them. They have a good mother. It's always the good parents that get the worst ungrateful ass kids. They hate me because of how I was born. As far as what I say, everyone says stupid things at times. Even they do. But it's not who I am to make someone feel stupid and I wouldn't talk about them behind their backs unless they did something to me.

I'm gone fix they smart asses and I know just how to do it.

The boys have a little shoot around in a few hours. I definitely

want them to go.

Thinking, thinking, thinking. When can I reveal to them what I'm gone do and it sting worse than a fucking bee?

Later today when it gets dark out again. Right before they go to bed. I don't care if they don't get not one ounce of sleep because shit. I'm not getting none tonight.

I'm smiling.

I don't like to get revenge, but I will. Especially if it's gone make me completely forget about what happened prior to make me want to seek it in the first place.

Takes me three hours to doze off because I'm so hurt behind the kids laughing as how I was born.

A lady once told me that people coming out with bushy eyebrows is natural. Some say I have bushy eyebrows because of my mother's poor choices. I know she loves liquor. Maybe she drank too much while I was in her. Maybe she took some pills she wasn't supposed to take. Whatever the case may be, I didn't ask to be like this and I thought my kids had enough sense to know that, or at least had a good enough heart to not talk bad about someone's eyebrows. Fuck them though.

My mother did not drink when she was pregnant with me.

I'm stressed the hell out and angry.

Chapter 32

I only get two hours of sleep before the alarm goes off. Mya arrives and I take the boys to basketball practice.

While I'm sitting in the stands, I'm trying to think of more I can do to piss of my kids. I'm so excited about tonight I can't really set my mind on anything else.

The entire time I'm in the gym people are looking at me, laughing, smiling, and whispering to each other. I am completely embarrassed and uncomfortable. I don't know why my kids have said about me to them.

The boys shoot around for an hour before huddling up and being released.

"See you tomorrow," Coach Eric says with a huge smile on his face. He knows his team is about to beat some ass. I smile back at him.

"Okay," I say.

Coach Eric doesn't have a care in the world about the shit my boys said and laughed at about me. I know they talk bad about me to him. If they'll do it in my house, then for sure they will tell other people.

Coach Eric is pretty much saying damn my kids disrespecting they momma. It's all about winning the games and keeping that number one spot. I know he's heard everything by now. The Rogers kids are the number on trending topic on every damn site. The headlining story on every blog. But he's just the coach right? All he's supposed to do is coach. Not worry about me, the mother of his two famous players.

I don't care though. I'm still gone do what I plan to do. I don't give a fuck about no one right now.

Justin and Josia kiss me on the forehead as we head out. They're so excited the entire car ride.

"I'm ready," Justin says referring to the next game.

I'm smiling at him through the rearview mirror.

"What about you Mom?" Justin asks.

I just keep smiling at him.

"Are you proud of us Momma?" Josiah asks.

I nod my head yes.

Back at the house the girls are watching TV with Mya. I only have thirty minutes to relax before I take Alisa to her dance practice. Her squad is performing again. They already had a different routine prepared because let's be real, they knew they would be going to the championship game.

"Hi mama," Charise says when I walk in the door. She runs up to me and gives me a hug.

"Hey," I say.

I sound so fake. I know Charise can tell, but I'm sure she thinks I'm just worn down. I'm making me a sandwich before I go. I pull out the bread and here is Alisa right next to me. She's so happy. Unfortunately I don't see her beauty anymore. She takes the bread out my hands.

"I'll make it for you Momma," Alisa says.

I let her.

After I eat, me and Alisa head right back to the gym.

"Mom can you go grab an ice cream or something?" Alisa asks at the gym.

"Why?" I ask.

"I don't want you to see this routine until tomorrow," Alisa says. "Please Mommy."

I don't say anything.

Alisa gives me a kiss on the forehead and says, "Love you Mom. Bye."

"Hi Ms. Leah," a few of her teammates say by the gym door.

I smile not wanting to open my mouth.

I don't want no damn ice cream so I pull into a parking space.

My face is just as jolly as ever as I grip the steering wheel.

I'm back to thinking of more ways to hurt my damn kids without touching them.

My phone vibrates.

It's a picture message from Lanice. It's an old picture of her kissing my forehead. The caption reads: *I love you.* I toss the phone in the passenger seat.

I'm nodding my head. Yes indeed. I'm cutting their phones off. The question is when can I go to the store to tell them when I want them damn mobile phones off or put on standby at least. I want to be strategic though. I think the best thing would be to have them cut off tomorrow morning.

I start the ignition and take my ass to the LA Call store and make it happen.

On the ride home Alisa asks me if we can stop to get something to eat.

"No," I say.

"Please Momma," Alisa says with her forced sad face. I used to think it was genuine.

"Not today. Tomorrow we can," I lie.

I'm not treating her ass nowhere.

Light bulb just went off in my head. I got another idea. I'm going to let the food in the house keep getting less, and I'm not buying no more snacks, candy or juice. I'm not gone buy no condiments whatsoever. Happy my lil' Alisa just asked that.

I was gone talk to the kids as little as possible until tonight, but maybe I should create some conversations so they'll give me more ideas. I don't want to hear they voices too much though so I'm going to chill in my room until tonight.

I pay Mya and she heads out.

Now I'm sitting up on my bed trying to see the best approach to telling the kids the news. The eviler side of me wants to just tell them what it is, but I think I want to let them know what I heard. Yea. I'm going to have to do that. I want them to know that now I see who they really are. I know what they honestly think of me.

"Hey Mom," Josiah says and comes in and gives me a hug.

94

"Hey Son," I say.

I take a deep breath. Let's see if I can get something out of him.

"Son is there something you want to tell me?" I ask.

Josiah slowly lets me go.

"Yes," Josiah says. I think he's about to admit to me his problem with his mother. I'm still gone say and do what I want to do tonight, but at least I will respect him for being honest. Josiah is smiling and looking me dead in my straight face.

"I love you," Josiah says. He kisses my forehead and sits on my bed.

"I'm about to take a nap Son," I say.

"Alright Mom," Josiah says. He hugs me again.

"Close the door please," I say.

Josiah's acting like he has no clue he did something; he's questioning why I would ask him if he had anything he wanted to tell me. My son is smart. But whatever. I'm going to get mines tonight. I need this damn time to scurry on along.

After watching a little TV I fall into a deep sleep. Damn.

When I wake up, I put some mouthwash in my mouth and call Josiah.

"I need you to tell everyone to come in my room," I say.

My attitude right now and ever since I heard their bullshit is *fuck these kids*.

Everyone comes in and stands around my bed.

"What's wrong Son?" I ask Josiah.

He doesn't say anything. Now here they all are and my ass is at a loss for words. I don't know how I want to begin.

"Are you okay Mommy?" Bianca asks.

"Would you guys ever disrespect me to your friends?" I ask.

They all say no serious as fuck and with the quickness. No one is telling on themselves with their eyes. Maybe they don't disrespect me to their friends.

"What about to each other?" I ask.

"No," Bianca lies.

Josiah says, "Mom we're really sorry. That night we just…" He doesn't know what to say. "We're sorry. Please forgive us."

All my kids are nodding their heads. I know they don't think they getting off that easy. I want to know more before I break the news to them.

My heart is racing so fast I don't know what I should tackle first. Let's start with Vayda's abusive ass video being deleted out my phone. I'm looking long and hard at Charise who now looks angry. I want to ask her why she deleted it, but I already heard her say why last night. I'm still gone ask anyways.

"Why did you go through my phone and delete my shit?" I ask.

Charise is at a loss for words.

"Vayda's beautiful and you don't like your ugly mother," I say caressing one of my eyebrows. "Damn that little boy she hit. Vayda just looks so good so she can do whatever she wants. I mean after all, she can take some nice pictures that don't need to be altered."

They know I'm now questioning any and everything nice they have ever said and done for me since they've been of age.

"Are you embarrassed by me Charise?" I ask. "You don't like me? You wish I was dead because I was born different?"

Charise shakes her head no to all of my questions and says no after the last one.

"Bianca come here," I say. She walks slowly to my bedside.

"I want you to show me what you were doing last night that had them laughing," I continue.

Bianca is crying.

"Mommy I'm sorry," Bianca says.

"Do I!" I yell.

Bianca cries no. I yell do it again and frighten her. She jumps back, then pulls her eyebrow hairs and walks like a hunchback in a circle. No one's laughing, but Charise smirks.

"That's funny huh Charise?" I ask.

Charise straightens up and stops laughing.

"Why aren't all y'all laughing?" I ask. "It was funny last night. Alisa, Justin and Josiah. Y'all are my oldest three. I thought if anyone would defend me to people, family or not, it would be you three. I was waiting on one of y'all to put Charise in her place. I definitely wasn't expecting you to be laughing. I'm your mother."

None of them say anything. They all look disappointed. Bianca trips and hurts her arm on the floor. She walks to me in tears. I take her hurting arm and turn her around.

"I don't want you up under me," I say. "Hell, I don't even want you near me."

The nerve of this damn girl to think someone she's hurting internally wants to comfort her. She's hurting me yet wants me to make her feel better about her arm.

"I stopped writing, doing seminars, going out, just fucking enjoying things I like to do on the daily so that you guys could pursue these damn careers and what happens?" I ask. "You get sucked up into this fame world that the mother you once loved feelings no matter. It's all about what the world thinks and does. Do you think the world's gone lose any sleep if you die tomorrow?"

All my kids look stupid as fuck.

"I'm only in my twenties!" I yell. "Do you really think I want to stop doing what I'm doing for a bunch of filthy, pathetic fucking kids?"

I have to stop for a minute and catch my breath. I'm on the brink of a heart attack.

"You know all I have to do is get rid of one of you and I can take one car and not need anyone's help to get from point A to point B," I say. "Charise you are one bad day away from getting put out my house. Believe me I don't care if you sleep on the streets right now. I can't believe all the shit that came out of your

mouth. This shit is fucking ridiculous. All my damn kids hate me."

"We don't Momma," Alisa says.

I want to vent more but I can't remember everything. My adrenaline is high.

Chapter 33

It's time. But I'm about to have some fun.

"Get out," I say after the meeting in my room.

I see Charise and Lanice smirk on their way out. I hear someone laugh too in the hallway. They think this shit is cute. They're probably thinking, *oh what's the worst Mommy is going to do to us?* They think I'm not gone do shit. They got me fucked up.

Once they all get out of my room, I call them back. They stand by the door. Josiah looks like he's trying to wipe the smirk off his face now. And so does Stacey. Oh I see how they roll now. Which is why I'm about to get they asses.

"Come back in," I say. They surround my bed again. They've all managed to put back on their serious faces after a few swallows of spit.

"Charise where's your phone?" I ask.

"In my room," Charise nervously says.

"Go get it," I say.

All of my kids look worried. I follow behind Charise. She grabs her phone off her bed and I snatch it from her.

"Put the passcode in," I say.

Charise must fucking think I'm completely stupid. She's tried three times and keeps failing.

"Hello!" I shout at her. "Did you forget it? What's in that phone that you don't want me to see? I want to now which pictures, collages, word phrases, whatever shit you are responsible for putting out there to the world."

A tear rolls down Charise's face. I don't care.

"You have less than a few seconds to tap me into that phone or I'm going to cut your hair," I say.

Charise is still trying. I walk out her room. I go in the hallway and rush back at her. She puts in the code. I knew her stupid ass would remember it once I walked out so she could delete

whatever bullshit she got going. I yank her phone out her hand and she rushes to the bathroom and locks the door.

Charise can't face me.

Once I get on Charise's *FriendSpot* account I know why. She has an entire account dedicated to pictures that ridicule my eyebrows. All types of collages with animals and shit. I scroll back to the tip. This accounts been active for three months. Two hundred and thirty six pictures. I want to strangle her ugly ass.

I'm browsing Charise's pictures and messages now. Even though I'm angry, a little happiness jumps back inside of me. She has the video of Vayda hitting her son. Of course it's private.

I'm watching the clip. Vayda's screaming and hollering at her son Antwon. She keeps pulling him harshly as she walks towards the front desk of the hotel. When the receptionist steps out to do something for her, she yanks his arm and he falls to the floor. Lil' man is crying bad.

I didn't intentionally record the video. I thought I was taking a photo of myself by the wall while I was waiting for someone to get me another key to my room. I didn't even know it was Vayda because she had on a hoody and glasses. It wasn't until I went home and showed Charise and Mya that I knew it was her. All I was thinking was thank goodness when I realized it was in fact her because I couldn't find any pictures of her son.

I knew I would wait on the perfect day to release that shit. I was waiting on a day that the media would rip her apart and I would add fuel to the fire. There were two times I could've done it if I had the footage on me. Once was when she got arrested for DUI and another was when she announced she had a miscarriage. Surely people would be grateful that another child didn't have to put up with this abusive bitch.

I'm wiggling the bathroom door.

"Come out Charise!" I yell.

"Mommy I'm sorry," Charise cries.

"Oh really!" I yell. "Are you sorry for hurting me or sorry

you just got caught!?"

"Both," Charise says.

I'm still wiggling the door with urgency and force. She won't come out.

"Charise I need to talk to all of you," I say. "I need you to come back in my room. I'm not going to do nothing to you. Have I ever?"

I go back in my room and sit on my bed. Everyone looks scared. Josiah looks like he's anticipating what I'm about to say.

"I'm waiting on Charise," I say. I've never looked so mean at these kids.

"You guys will be standing here all night," I continue.

Josiah goes to the bathroom and tells Charise to come out, ashamed as fuck. My eyes stare deathly at her as she walks in front of my bed.

"What did I do to deserve this?" I ask.

"Nothing Mom," Alisa says.

She's trying to sound remorseful.

"We're just stupid kids that messed up," Alisa continues.

"Damn," I say. "Just when we were doing so well you guys show me exactly who you are, which is not kids that I would be proud putting out to the world. I expect you guys to defend me, not talk bad about me."

"We're really sorry Mom," Justin says.

Josiah is my oldest. I'm the most disappointed in him. Of them all, he's the one that always shows me the most love and now I don't think he meant any of it.

I'm looking at Charise.

"You know all this time I thought it was the world that was belittling me," I say. "Making me feel worthless. Making me not want to leave the house because I knew more and more jokes would be made, and my own damn daughter is doing it before I can even walk out the damn door! Pull up your personal account or is this your only one?"

101

Charise pulls up her main account and look at that, not a single picture of me on it. But guess who she's in all types of collages with? Vayda.

"She could be my mommy," I read out loud from one of her posts.

I move my head towards Josiah.

"You guys knew about the account and didn't tell her to take it down," I say with tears. "If I'd have known you guys were that embarrassed by me I would've worn my hair down every day."

My tears stop when I realize I'll get the last laugh out of this shit. I'm laughing now. I'm just as devilish as I want to be right now. They're staring at me trying to figure out where my joy comes from. Before I get the ultimate revenge, I got one thing I need to have done.

"Bring me your phones and computers," I say.

I follow Lanice and Alisa. I suspect them more of having bullshit about me in their phones than the boys. I go through all their pictures. They watch me the entire time. Charise is the only one that has hurtful pictures of me.

"I want *FriendSpot* and *ChitChatFam* accounts deleted right now," I say. "Bring me the computers too."

Hold on. I have an idea. I have Charise delete every post about me and make public the video of Vayda mistreating her son.

Charise's account only has two thousand followers, but when it comes to celebrity gossip, people become more interested in people fast.

I wish I could see the look on that bitch Vayda's face when people tell her what used to be on Charise's account before the video of her surfaced.

This is the only account I let Charise leave up.

"What's the password Charise?" I ask.

She doesn't want to say.

"What is it!?" I scream.

"Leah Rogers," Charise says.

I'm going to log into the account on my phone. I want to be alerted of my messages, comments, and likes. I'm ready to watch this bitch Vayda crumble. I can't wait to hear what her ditzy ass says when she's questioned by interviewers.

Alisa looks like she's ready to crumble. I'm staring at her trying to figure out why she looks like any minute she's going to explode.

I look Josiah square in his eyes.

"You're not playing in the game tomorrow," I say.

Yep. That's right. He worked hard all summer to not play in the most important game he'd ever play in.

"What!" Josiah yells, pissed.

"Neither are you Justin," I say.

"You made us do all that work for nothing?!" Josiah yells.

"That's exactly what I did, and guess what Alisa?" I say.

She's tearing up.

"Forget that fucking half-time show," I say.

I'm laughing and smiling.

All my kids are serious as a heart attack.

Chapter 34

I turn the TV on.

"Let's see what everyone is saying about the game tomorrow," I say.

I'm skimming through the channels looking for a news station.

Wait. Something looks a little all too familiar. One of these fucking dumb, idiot, bitch-ass kids forgot to turn off their webcam. They're little gathering last night is on TV.

The reporter is talking.

You've got to feel sorry for Leah right now. I mean these kids definitely disrespected her the worst they possibly could. But let's hope that she can move past this and just support them at their game tomorrow. Tons of celebrities are going out to see these kids play. These young kids get a lot of playing time on a team comprised of high school kids and led them to an undefeated season. If these kids win tomorrow they go to nationals which is held in New York this year. They have a chance to be number one in the country.

I can't believe this shit. They've embarrassed me publicly.

The reporter continues.

They must've just had a bad night. We see these kids all the time with their mother and they do genuinely love her.

Alisa looks at me. "Yes Mom. We do," she struggles to say through her pain.

The TV is showing footage of me and the kids walking around town.

The reporter laughs as she says:

I think they just were up late and got bored and unfortunately their mother became the topic.

I shut the TV off.

I am fucked.

Now on top of me knowing who these kids really are, so does the entire world.

That's not what has me wanting to commit homicide right now though. It's the fact that everyone's laughing at me. Whenever I leave the house and see someone laugh and smile at me, I'll think it's because of what these jackasses said. I should've had abortions.

"Did you guys mean to record it or was it left on, on accident?" I ask.

"I was video chatting with fans and I forgot to click out," Josiah admits.

"Everybody needs to call their coaches and let them know they won't be participating in anything until further notice," I say. "Get out."

Everyone leaves the room.

"Do you want me to shut the door Mom?" Alisa asks, crying.

"Yes," I say.

As soon as it's shut, I break down. I'm pressing my hands over my heart as tight as I can because it hurts so bad and feels like it's about to pop. I'm in pain. I'm controlling my breathing like a pregnant woman does during birth so I don't have a heart attack.

My life is ruined. There's no way my kids can make this up to me. They've done the worst thing they could possibly do. How can I be mad at the world laughing and making jokes about me when my own kids do? I don't like how that bitch on the news was more concerned with the fucking game as opposed to the behavior of the boys.

I log into *FriendSpot* to see what everyone is saying. People are responding *lol* and *lmao* to the news report links with the video the kids made.

No one cares about me.

Because these kids look good and have talent, what they do

doesn't matter. Good looks to this generation means that you can do whatever you want and nothing bad should happen to you.

Well I'm gone break that shit in my kid's minds. They'll think twice about fucking with me again.

I'm about to go see what they doing.

Bianca and Stacey are playing with toys in their room. The other girls aren't in theirs. Josiah and Justin's door is locked. I bang on it.

"Open this damn door!" I yell.

Charise opens it.

"Girl's go to your damn room," I say.

They're all staring at me with their demonized faces like I'm the one that did something wrong. I follow behind them laughing. I feel good. I know this rush is only going to last so long though. I need to think of something else to piss them off.

"Put the toys away and go to bed," I demand Stacey and Bianca.

Bianca hits her elbow on the wall. I grab the arm with the hurting elbow and direct her away from me. That shit must've really hurt, but I don't want her up under me. I don't even want her near me right now.

"Girls y'all better take y'all asses to bed too," I say.

Just like I never witnessed their foul language, they never witnessed mine; but they gone hear a lot more of it.

"Raggedy bitches," I mumble as I walk back to my room.

I know they heard me.

I turn my alarm off for tomorrow. No need to wake up early since I don't got nowhere to go. I feel released. Basketball season's too damn long anyways. I don't think I'm letting them play for a couple years. Hell, I could strip them of playing or doing any damn thing until they're eighteen and out my house. Then I could laugh at them.

They really fucked with me the wrong way.

I put a pillow in between my legs and fall asleep marinating

on the negative things could do to pay these kids back.

Once something's on the internet, it's there forever.

Even if someone were to delete all the videos, there's those people that have saved them to their computers and will upload them again when they think no one is thinking about it.

My kids have ruined my life and now it's my turn to make them pay for it. How long I will restrict them, I don't know. But I do know it will be a lengthy amount of time. If I never get past this shit, then they won't be doing a damn thing until they're eighteen and out of my house.

I'm searching through Alisa's phone looking for answers to why she looked deathly when I had it in my possession. The pictures aren't giving me a reason, so I'm going to call all her contacts that I don't know.

I dial someone named Lucy and a male voice answers.

"Who's this?" I ask.

He hangs up.

"Alisa!" I yell.

"Yes," Alisa cries.

"Who's Lucy?" I ask.

"A high school boy," Alisa says.

She stored a boy under a girl's name just in case I went through her phone.

"And what are you doing with this high school boy?" I ask.

"We kiss sometimes and I…" Alisa's hesitant. "I sucked him a couple times."

"Lil' girl get out my face," I say.

Before I go to bed, Josiah asks me to give them a different punishment.

"Please. Anything else Mom," Josiah sadly says.

"Get out my room," I say and slam the door behind him.

Kids picking their punishment? That shit is unheard of.

My phone beeps. There's twenty comments already on Vayda's video. The one I like the most is: *Calls CPS.* Yes.

107

Whoever wrote that probably won't, but I know this video will make the news. And after flipping through a few channels it's there. Police are already parked outside her house. But she's not home. Go figure. The news reporter is saying that her son might get taken away from her. They have a bunch of unanswered questions and I'm just sitting back laughing as they try to figure out the answers.

The rest of the night I sip wine and read comments about Vayda. People are already doing vlogs about the situation. Celebrities are posting statuses with Vayda's name tagged in them. It's on and poppin' now. The police will have to do something. That bitch can't hide forever.

Payback is a bitch.

I sleep good.

Chapter 35

I use the bathroom, then go check on my two irritating ass munchkins, Bianca and Stacey. They're not in their room. Neither are the other girls.

The house is silent and everyone is usually up at this time.

I go to the boy's room and the door is locked. I bang on it before putting my ear to the door. It's silent as hell. I take a knife and unlock the door.

No ones in the room.

I couldn't get to my room fast enough to grab the phone off the charger.

It's not there, and I'm positive I put it on the charger.

I'm searching high and low for it.

I can't find it. I'm looking for my purse now. It's nowhere to be found. Neither are my car keys that I think I sat right next to it on my nightstand.

Maybe I locked them in the car. Nope. The ignition is empty, but I do have a flat tire that I'm sure I didn't have yesterday.

I'm in the driveway pacing back and forth.

I don't know what to do right now.

I go back to my room and turn on the TV and there my boys are on the damn court playing basketball. Alisa's on the sideline cheering. Coach Eric calls a timeout and the camera surveys the audience. There my fucking other kids are sitting in the stands. Those fucking no good ass kids.

Question after question is floating through my mind. I know the boys probably rode the bus, but how did the girls get there? How did the boys get to the school? Who the fuck helped them out?

I'm about to ask the neighbors to use their phone. It's not until I'm let in that I realize I don't have my phone with the kid's numbers in it.

"Everything okay?" the lady of the house, Ms. Chelsea asks

when she opens the door.

"Yes," I say. I start to walk out but she stops me.

"My kids and husband are at the game," Ms. Chesea says with concern.

It's clear as day that she wants to know what's going on. Why am I not there? At the game. Most importantly why did I go to her house if I didn't want nothing? I don't even care to explain nothing.

"Thanks for supporting them," I say. "I'm not feeling well so I will go on home."

"Anything I can do?" Ms. Chelsea asks worried.

"No," I say and go home.

I don't want my neighbors knowing my business.

I'm walking all over my place trying to figure out what I want to do. These kids have disobeyed me in a huge way. And I feel like I have no control over my youngest two.

I have no choice.

I'm getting rid of them. My oldest five.

That's foul.

I'm not going to make any phone calls, or post any statuses.

I'm looking up the address right now on my computer of a foster care place and I'm going to drive them down there personally and drop them off. They won't see it coming.

After jotting down everything I need to know for the little excursion, I tune into the game.

My boys look like they don't have a care in the world about me. Just that fucking first place trophy. They have to win first in order to make it to the tournament in New York.

I wonder if they really think I would let they asses go to that shit considering what the fuck they did today. Probably. They probably thought of something to get on the damn flight. I want the fucking camera to show my girls again. It doesn't, but it's half-time.

Alisa is all smiles as she moves her lil' body to the music with

her crew.

The boys end up winning. My girls rush over to them on the court. They don't have an ounce of remorse or fear in them.

I'm gone show they asses when I drop them off. I can't wait for them to walk through this fucking door.

Think I'll play it cool today because I need to call CPS to make sure I'm doing everything right. I don't want no mistakes. I want them gone.

I hop in the shower and pull myself together. I'm trying to find comfort in the fact that today is the last day these kids will disappoint me. I wrap a towel around me and go in my room.

Fuck. Something just hit my window. I open the blinds. It's hailing. The fuck is up with this bipolar ass weather? It was just sunny out. Another piece of hail hits the window. This shit is coming down faster and faster. It's hailing and raining. This shit is all fucking bad.

I put on some clothes and sit downstairs on the couch. I'm hoping the kids will show up any second, but as the weather gets worse, I know that's not gone happen.

I pour myself some wine and sit the glass bottle on the living room table. I drink the entire bottle.

I don't know where my kids are or it they're alright. The cable is out so I don't know if the team even made it back this way. Sometimes they stay and watch other games or go out to eat.

I honestly don't care if my oldest five are alright. Just my youngest two.

I go through another bottle of wine and try to sleep, but I can't because this weather is off the chain. It literally sounds like someone is throwing rocks at my window.

I'm walking back and forth in my room. Well, stumbling back and forth in my room. I drunk way too damn much.

But at least I'm at ease.

It's not like the kids are coming today.

Chapter 36

I was gone fix me something to eat, but I can't tell if I'm hearing things or if my garage door really is sliding up. I hear voices too, but they're definitely not the sound of my kids.

I lock my room door and shut the light off as I listen to figure out how many people just broke in my house.

"Look all over while you so damn ready to take the damn TV," I hear a man say. "They probably got some better stuff in here."

My hand is over my mouth. I'm scared as fuck. I feel for my charger, then remember I don't have a phone.

"Check that room over there," a different man says.

Someone's wiggling my door. I silently go to my bathroom and shut the door.

"Fuck the door's locked," someone says.

I'm sitting on the toilet.

Hold up. I hear something. He's using a knife to get in my room. Fuck. He's trying to come in the bathroom.

"The fuck is wrong with this family locking all the damn doors," someone says.

I have no idea how many people are in my house.

"It's locked because someone's in there," the first man I heard talk says.

"Man ain't nobody in there," someone says. "You see that damn weather. Them niggas not gone be here tonight. We can sleep here if we want."

I'm trying to find something to fight these bastards with.

"You owe me," someone says.

Someone's kicking the door. I turn the light on. I grab a spray bottle of bleach. I turn the light back off and stand next to the wall so when the door opens I'm behind it.

Someone gets in and turns the light on. I spray him with bleach and he screams like hell. I was about to spray his friend,

but he has a gun pointed at me.

"Drop the bottle and go next to the sink," the man that has the gun pointed at me says.

His friend is still screaming at the top of his lungs. He helps him get water in his eyes and passes him a dry towel to put pressure on them.

"Please take what you want and go," I say.

"Oh I'm gone take a lot you bitch," the man I squirted with bleach say and then slaps me to the floor.

"Now just what the fuck are we gone do with this bitch?" one of the other men say.

The man I squirted grabs my arm and pulls me to the bed. I resist as much as I can.

"Get out," the man I squirted with bleach says.

I try to make a run for it to the door but the man with the gun points it at my forehead again.

"Behave," the man with the gun says to me. "And nah," he says to the man I squirted with bleach. "I'm grabbing a chair and watching."

"Grab me something to tie her damn arms together," the man I squirted with bleach says.

"Use your big ass arm," the gunman says and leaves the room. Now this big ass man, the man I squirted with bleach, is pulling down my shorts. He grabs me super tight and bends me over on the bed. He pulls my panties down, finds the hole and plunges his penis right inside of me.

I'm crying like hell.

"You fucking bitch. You gone spray me with bleach. Fuck you," he says cockily.

He's going relay fast in and out of me now. He's moaning and enjoying raping me. After a couple minutes he pulls out and cums on my bed. He flips me over and licks my vagina up and down.

"Where them pretty little girls at?" the man I squirted with

bleach asks laughing. "I'd do them boys too."

The gunman has yet to come back up, and there's nothing in my reach to hit his friend with or throw at my window. He's eating me like he's been starved.

I hear a few voices coming down the hallway.

"Let me get in that," the newcomer demands.

"Matt fuck you," the man I squirted says as he continues to devour me. The newcomer yanks his head back and he gets up.

The newcomer wipes my private area with the bed sheet.

"Help!" I yell.

The newcomer slaps me.

"Nobody's gone hear you," the newcomer says as he puts duct tape over my mouth and ties my hands together. He eats me for a few seconds then goes in and out of me with his dick while the man I squirted with bleach jacks off. The newcomer stays in my vagina for a few pumps then tries to go in my ass. This shit hurts like hell. He's stretching me out as fast as he can. The other perverts come in and watch.

I have four men watching this one rape me.

"Somebody needs to go back and watch the car," my first rapist, the man I squirted with bleach, says.

"You forgot your brother rolled with us," the gunman says. "He on the phone right now. If anybody make they way here we gone know in advance. We got someone on every corner."

One of the other men is grabbing my titties while one of his crew members keeps going in and out my vagina. I want to die right now.

"Did we come here to come up or just nut?" the gunman asks.

"Come up," the man I squirted with bleach says. "But since she here, we might as well nut."

The man I squirted with bleach is laughing still jacking off.

I have multiple men going in and out of me. They even put two dicks in me at once. They gang bang me all night.

To conclude their raping session with me, they all nut inside

114

of me. They don't stop until three in the morning. Now I have my first rapist cuddling me from behind with his penis inside me going to sleep. He sporadically goes in and out all night.

I can't believe this shit.

Chapter 37

My ears are alert with this jackass still cuddling me.

Sounds like the rest of the men are in my kitchen eating.

I hear the gunman in the hallway saying it's supposed to hail for the next three days. I just know they're going to kill me. There's no way they're going to get me inside a car willingly. If my hands get free again, I'm running. I don't care if I get shot.

I finally manage to fall asleep.

I'm woke up by bath water the next day. I was hoping the hail would stop but it doesn't.

My first rapist puts me in the tub. He bathes me, dries me off, then fucks me in the bathroom. The boys take turns with me all day. I'm doing everything I can to remember the faces of these bastards.

I want my sons to rescue me so bad. I heard everything they said. They didn't know I was around and they didn't know a camera was rolling. There's just no way they could convince me they were just playing around. I feel like I've been a fool for so long. But if they save me, I will feel a lot better.

I'm worried as hell about my two youngest kids. I wonder if they were lied to or if they left the house being disobedient as well. I can't look nothing past any of them after hearing all that bullshit that night I stood by the door.

I expect the worst from my kids from now on. My dreams are full of hate for them as well as the hate they have for me.

I keep having visuals of me cutting my girls precious long hair on stage in front of a huge crowd of people. Dreams of me pulling them off stage right when they walk on to embarrass them and let their hard work go down the drain. Dreams of me putting them out with poisoned food or something and them getting kidnapped. Dreams of them going through rape just like I am now.

Then my dreams shift to things they would and could do to

me because they hate me so much. I see them mixing bleach in with my alcohol. Spitting in my water. Cutting my clothes up. Messing with me while I'm in a deep sleep.

The worst dream is Alisa sleeping with a grown man she knew I liked. I just don't look anything past them now. They're very good actors. I can see them doing a lot more things I would never expect.

These are my thoughts the following days while being gang banged and raped.

Chapter 38

The hail has slowed down a little. I'm certain by now these criminals have come up with some type of better strategy to get rid of me.

"Aye, pick her up and bring her downstairs," the gunman says to rapist number one.

When rapist number one tosses me on the couch like I'm nothing, I look around and notice it's just us three in the house.

The gunman goes in the garage.

"You know you pretty bitches don't know what you're missing when you don't fuck wit' niggas like me," rapist one vents. "You liked that shit huh?"

He's walking around my living room now looking at pictures of my kids. He picks up a recent one of Alisa and kisses it three times.

"I wish she was here," rapist one says smiling at me.

He picks up a picture of Josiah and shakes his head. He licks the photo. He's distracted staring at my kids.

I'm twisting and turning my hands trying to get this duct tape off. They have it on so tight I can't spot anything close that I could grab to get this shit off of me.

Rapist one is still distracted making love to my kid's pictures. Come on Leah. Find something. I'm talking to myself internally. I'm doing the best I can to feel in between the couch pillows for something.

I see a pen. I grab it when rapist one closes his eyes and starts kissing a picture. I'm poking at the tape.

Yes. I got a hole in it.

"Aye, look bitch," rapist one says.

He's rubbing a picture of Charise against his penis. I tuck the pen in between my legs. He places the picture back and paces the room looking down at the floor going on his rant about how women have always done him wrong. He barely looks at me

which is why I'm able to stretch the holes I made in the duct tape.

Fuck. I need to make a move and now before the gunman comes back. I can't take a chance on having to dodge two people.

Rapist one is looking out the peephole. I twist my wrists and my hands are released. I rush upstairs to my room. Rapist one makes it up but his big ass is too damn slow.

"Open up bitch!" rapist one screams.

I use my heels to break my glass window.

"Help!" I scream.

I see two cars parked across the street that I've never seen before. I hear the gunman at the door again.

I have to jump. I toss my pillows and sheets out the window.

The gunman is mad as hell going through their plans saying they were going to knock me out, put me in a trash bin and haul my ass to their trunk.

"Where's the gun?" rapist one asks.

"I left it in the car," the gunman says. "For some reason I thought I was just coming to clean up, not make a bigger mess."

I should've known they wouldn't shoot me. A bullet would definitely get the neighbors attention.

The gunman and rapist one barge in the door. My leg is only halfway out the window. I get both legs out but not fast enough to let go and fall. The gunman and rapist one drag me back in and throw me on the floor.

I'm screaming like hell. My arm hit the wall and is broken. On top of that, gunman and rapist one are kicking my stomach.

The gunman's phone rings. While he's listening to someone talk, rapist one is pulling down my shorts and preparing to fuck me another time.

The gunman hangs up the phone.

"We got to go," the gunman says. "Finish her off and come on," he continues and heads downstairs.

I'm still screaming my lungs out.

Rapist one still picks me up and goes inside me one last time. Once rapist one finishes inside me, he throws me against the wall again and punches my face repeatedly.

"See how many niggas you pull when I'm threw with you," rapist one says. "Why you screaming like that? You're arm hurt?"

He throws me to the ground and steps on my broken arm repeatedly, then uses his strength to break my other arm. He's laughing and the gunman is downstairs making a lot of noise. I hear glass breaking.

Rapist one goes to the window when he hears police sirens. They're getting louder and louder.

"Time for me to go bitch," rapist one says and puts his foot on my right thigh and fucks up my leg.

My visions getting blurry.

Chapter 39

Thought I was dead until I woke up in a hospital bed with a nurse. I can't see what she's doing. Both of my arms are in casts and so is my leg.

I'm crippled.

"Don't worry," the nurse says. "I'm prepping this for someone else."

She has a scalpel in her hand.

"You're lucky to be alive," the nurse says. "How do you feel?"

"How long have I been here?" I ask. "Oh, and I feel okay."

"Less than twenty-four hours," another nurse says walking in the room.

She's not dressed like a staff member though.

"Leah this is Angeleek," the nurse with the scalpel says. "She's an in -home nurse. I take it you don't want to remain here when you have kids to take care of right?"

"Right," I say. "I need to get home."

"Your wheelchair is being brought up right now," Angeleek says.

"Thanks," I say.

"I know you don't want to hear this right now, but the police are standing outside the door," the nurse with the scalpel says. "They want to come in and talk to you."

"Tell them to meet me at my house," I say. "I need to get there before my kids do."

Angeleek escorts me to her vehicle and drives me home. I'm angry as fuck. All this damn work to get out the car.

"It'll get better," Angeleek says to me.

Angeleek turns into a contradiction the second she opens my front door. My house is a fucking mess. Broken dishes all over the place. The people that broke in my house tore this shit up. My couch has been cut. My TV's gone, clothes are all over the

place. And this is what I see from the door view.

"Leave me right here," I say.

I want to stay right by the door.

"I'll make some room for you," Angeleek says.

"No," I say. "I want everything to remain just like it is. Cleaning up is not gone help any damn thing. Leave everything like it is."

"You know there's people that have made it through a lot worse than you," Angeleek says.

"Please be quiet," I say.

I am crippled and thinking about everything that's happened with the gunman and his crew. I'm picturing those jackasses ruining everything and stealing my shit.

There's blood trailing to the door.

The doorbell rings.

Angeleek lets the police in. They stand right in front of me.

"Ms. Rogers we caught the three men responsible for this," the policewoman says.

"Only three?" I ask.

"How many people were here?" the policeman asks.

"Five," I say. "But I still want to know where you found three of them?"

"Speeding out the neighborhood," the policeman says. "I thought it was very suspicious when I saw them coming from the direction I was headed at eighty miles an hour so I stopped them. One pulled a gun on me and I knew we had who we were looking for."

So they have rapist, the gunman and one of the other men.

"The doctors are doing more tests from the semen she swabbed off of you," the policewoman says. "Hopefully we can figure out who the other two men were."

"Can you wheel me in front of the couch?" I ask.

Angeleek gladly does.

"Have a seat," I tell the police.

"I'm going to get a few of your things out of my car," the policeman says.

He opens the door and in walks my disobedient seven children. First one is Bianca who cries instantly when she sees me. She walks right in front of me and stares. Everyone else slowly and guiltily make their way in front of me.

Josiah bends down and cries on my leg.

"Momma I'm so sorry," Josiah says.

Bianca is screaming and hollering.

"The TV said you were dead," Stacey cries.

The policeman brings in two of my TVs, the boy's game system, a couple pictures of my kids, and a suitcase. ON his last trip in he's trailed by a miserable looking Grace, Mrs. Claire and lastly Ron.

I know these son of a bitches weren't the fucking accomplices.

I kick my leg so Josiah's disrespectful ass can get away from me. He stands next to his siblings.

"Be quiet," I bitterly say to Bianca.

She lowers her voice.

"You guys are very lucky your mother's still alive," the policewoman says.

Both her and her male partner are looking at me stare at my children like I want to kill them. And right now I do.

"Whose idea was it?" I ask my kids.

No one says anything.

"Whose idea was it?" I ask my kids.

No one says anything.

"Whose! Fucking! Idea was it!" I ask my kids.

No one says anything.

"Whose! Fucking! Idea was it?" I ask louder.

"Ma'am we're going to follow up with you tomorrow," the policeman says and heads to the door. "Great game the other day," he says looking at Josiah and Justin.

"I need you to stay," I say. "Can you get me in contact with foster care?"

The officers along with Angeleek look puzzled. My children look so damn pathetic.

"We had no clue what the kids were up to Leah," Mr. Ron remorsefully says.

"Can I ask what's going on?" the policewoman asks.

I'm crying now and I can barely talk.

"Somebody tell her," I say to the kids.

None of them can fix their lips to say a thing. After a long silence I spit it out.

"The day of the game they snuck out, took my car keys, slit my tire and more," I say. "I grounded them for their behavior so they weren't supposed to attend the game. I would've called the coach the second I could, but his number was in my cell phone and I can't find it."

The cops and Angeleek are looking at the kids in disbelief.

"Mommy I'm so sorry," Alisa whines.

"Where's my damn keys?!" I scream.

Alisa pulls my purse out her cheerleading bag.

I can't believe this shit.

"Dump everything out of it on the table," I say.

My cell phone falls out.

"Sir can we speak to you outside?" the policewoman asks Mr. Ron.

"No," I say. "Please talk to him here so I can understand why he would take them anywhere without the okay from me."

"They called and said you weren't feeling well," Mr. Ron says. "That they needed a ride to the gym. We've never had a problem out of them. You yourself said they were reliable and trustworthy. I didn't think it was possible for all of them to get out the house without you knowing."

"We apologize," Mrs. Claire says.

"So you picked them up from here?" the policewoman asks.

"Yes," Mr. Ron says. "I drove the car and so did my oldest daughter and wife. I took the boys to the gym so t hey could ride with the team. I tried calling your phone but it went straight to voicemail, and I couldn't get through on the house phone either."

"Bianca and Stacey did they lie to you or did you willingly disobey Mommy?" I cry.

"We disobey you Mommy," Stacey cries.

"Are you sorry?" I ask.

"Yes," Stacey says.

"Okay. Mommy will keep you two," I say.

I look at my oldest kids.

"But I want them gone tonight," I say to the officers. "Alisa why did you take my phone?"

She doesn't say anything.

"Mr. Ron and Mrs. Claire and Grace please leave," I say.

I'm pissed at them, but it's not their fault. My kids had me fooled too. They aren't the saints I thought they were. Hopefully the Wallace's learn from this shit. Besides, they aren't the core of this. The kids sneaking out the house is. That's how all this shit came about.

"Mom I swear I'll do anything to fix this," Josiah cries.

I'm shaking my head. My fucking oldest is such a disappointment. I'm on hush mode right now. I'm waiting on these damn cops to make happen what I asked. I need so foster people to make they way to my damn address.

The Wallace's head out the door. Grace looks upset. Not because of what happened to me. Because she know she not gone see this trifling mutha fucka Justin again.

The policeman steps outside. He's making a phone call to someone. It better be foster care.

"It won't happen again," Lanice cries.

"I have to have someone take care of me for a while," I angrily say.

I'm beyond furious at this shit. I had to be put to sleep at the

damn doctor and that's shit I never wanted to do. I don't trust nobody. Somebody at that damn hospital could've raped my ass. Now I want everything that happened to me to happen to these kids.

"We can take care of you," Alisa says.

Lanice nods her head.

To be honest, I really don't' want this damn stranger wiping my ass and cat. But I do want these kids gone. I don't even know if I can trust them to do anything now. If someone loses my trust, they can never get it back.

The policeman comes back in with two older looking black women. My kids look terrified.

"Please Momma. Don't do this," Alisa cries. "It won't happen again."

I ignore her and drag my attention to my boys.

"You guys love a basketball and first place trophy more than your Mom?" I ask.

They both shake their heads no. Josiah kisses my forehead.

"Leah this is Mildred and Tiffany from foster care service," the policeman says. "Just say the word and they will escort the kids out."

The policeman is talking in a way that makes it obvious he doesn't want this to happen. I'm staring at my bold ass kids trying to figure out what's best for me. They look weak and scared now.

If they stay, they can help me and I would just let Angeleek supervise the house to ensure they don't got no plans of killing me. If they go, I'll have the last laugh knowing they're somewhere they don't want to be. If they stay I can think of something else to piss them off.

However, I think placing them in foster care will do it. Who knows, maybe I will forgive them. They'll probably make it up to me. How they will do that, I have no idea. I'm scarred for life.

As angry as I am, I still love these kids, but if they were to

pass away right now I wouldn't care.

"Mildred," I say.

Before I can continue Josiah cuts me off.

"I'll never play basketball again," Josiah says.

I'm looking in his eyes. He means it. He's on his knees by my messed up leg.

"Mommy I love you," Josiah says. "I, we messed up and I promise we will do any and everything to make it up to you. Don't give up on us."

I can't believe this bastard.

"What do you mean you will never play basketball again?" I ask.

He just alerted my brain what would've postponed that call to foster care. Nationals are coming up.

"You are going to play in those games," I say. "You'll sneak out again, right? Otherwise all of this would've been for nothing."

Josiah's shaking his head no.

"That's what this is about right?" I ask. "An undefeated season? A first place trophy?"

"I love you more than basketball Mom," Josiah says.

"Let me tell you two something," I say to my two boys. "You're either going to play in those games and practice up to that time, or everyone's leaving tonight."

"Do you want us to play in them?" Justin asks.

"Does it really matter what I want Justin?" I ask. "But if you must know, yes. Crippled and all I want to find a way to New York and watch you guys play. I want to watch you win what's so precious and priceless to you. What's worth your mom being raped by multiple men. What's worth making me stranded and without a phone to call for help. I want to attend."

"You guys can go," I say to Mildred and Tiffany. "I'll call you in a few weeks."

"We'll be contacting you," the policeman says as him and his partner follow the foster care people out the house.

Chapter 40

My bladder is acting up.

"Alisa help me to the bathroom," I say.

I want to see if she's even capable of taking care of me.

"Here. Let me help you," Angeleek says. "It's gone take more than one person."

They both pull my shorts and panties down, help me get on the toilet, then start to leave. I stare at Alisa angrily and mad as hell this stranger is seeing all my damn privates.

"Stay Alisa," I say.

I stare at her the entire time I'm sitting on the toilet.

I'm finished for a good thirty seconds before I inform her that she needs to grab the tissue and wipe my ass like I'm a damn child.

"Go get Angeleek," I say when Alisa finishes wiping me.

They both wheel me back in the living room.

The kids are straightening up the house. It's gone take them all night to get this place back together.

Charise is cleaning up my trail of blood.

I want to go in my damn room.

"Can you help me hop up the stairs Angeleek?" I ask.

"That's not a good idea," Angeleek says. "You don't want to take a chance on falling with that cast on."

"I been through a lot of pian this week," I say. "Believe me when I say falling won't hurt me one bit. Justin and Josiah?"

"Yes Mom?" Josiah answers.

"I need you guys to help me up the stairs," I say.

I hop step by step up to my room and lay back on my bed. This is more like it.

"You need anything else Mom?' Josiah asks.

"Turn on the TV and make me a sandwich please," I say.

Josiah does as he is told.

"Turn to the news," I say.

The boys are disgusted and I am angry as fuck.
There we are.

The reporter named April says:

We're hearing now that they may have snuck out the house.

"Go downstairs," I say.

April continues.

Leah's house was broken into. She was raped by multiple men, and is crippled at the moment.

There's footage of me being escorted out the hospital.

April continues:

She's in a two story house. If she heard the men come in, you would think she had plenty of time to make a call, get somewhere and hide. Grab a weapon. Something. Most of us want to know why she didn't attend her kid's game. Some are speculating that she may have not given them permission to go, but I have a hard time seeing seven kids sneak out of the house. Especially with those two little ones. Zen, don't you think they would've at least left the two youngest girls?

The camera switches to Zen.

Well April, we just got word that the kids did not in fact have permission to play in that game. They lied to their coaches as well as the people, who we now know are the Wallace's, who helped them get from point A to point B. The criminals knew the boys had a game that day and assumed their entire family was there. Once the weather got bad they knew everyone would be stranded for a while and that's why they made the move they did. This is definitely a heartbreaking story. I'm sending it back to you April.

April speaks again.

Thanks Zen. You know the most disappointing fact is that if the kids were there, especially her sons, this wouldn't have gotten as bad as it did for their mother. This story is such a disheartening one. Here is this family full of potential billion dollar kids and they do something that ruins their image completely. There's definitely a lot of unanswered questions that the public wants to know? I'm going to send it over to you George.

A reporter named George speaks:

Thanks April. As far as image goes, if the mother recuperates and does not become mentally ill like so may other people that have been raped, molested, whatever the case may be, and if the kids stay out of the limelight for a minute and the family becomes as close as they were, or maybe they still are, we don't know, I believe they can come bac out with a bang. I don't think their careers will have a meltdown. These are kids we're talking about. Everyone goes through their rough times with their kids.

April pops back up.

Thanks George. Well folks, we are definitely hoping the famous Rogers can get through this and be back on the map soon.

I shut the TV off. That bitch is pressing me. First off, what the fuck does she mean *'the public wants to know more details of what happened'?* Like it's their damn business. I can't stand this bullshit. I don't like that I'm still under the impression that this world doesn't give a damn about what I went through. All they care about is my good looking ass kids continuing on with their careers and staying in the limelight.

"Here you go Mom," Josiah says and gives me my sandwich.

I'm tearing up looking at him. He walks out and slowly turns around when he reaches the hallway. He feeds me my sandwich. My tears are still rolling because I feel he's remorseful and truly

regrets what's happened.

"Get me some water please," I say to Josiah.

I only take a few sips because I don't want to work hard just to get on the toilet again.

After I eat, I have Josiah get me my small mirror out the bathroom drawer. Now I know where all the blood came from. My damn face. I got two big knots on my forehead and my cheeks are real swollen. I look back at my son who's tearing up again.

"I'm going to kill who did this to you Mom," Josiah says.

"Call Coach Eric and tell him you need a ride tomorrow," I say to Josiah, completely ignoring what he just said.

Coach Eric wants to speak to me. Go fucking figure. Josiah holds the phone to my ear.

"Hello?" I say.

"How you doing Ms. Leah?" Coach Eric asks. "Josiah said he needs a ride to practice tomorrow?"

"Yes he does," I say.

"Okay. I'll have one of his teammates come get him," Coach Eric says.

"Sounds good," I say.

"Hang up the phone," I say to Josiah.

He's cleaning my room now. There's broken glass and blood on the floor. I watch my sons every move. I'm just now remembering that I'm sitting in this filthy ass bed I was gang raped in.

Where do I want to go in this house? Definitely not in the kids room.

"I need you to help me back downstairs," I say to Joisah.

Josiah gets Justin and they put me on the recliner in the living room.

Angeleek is still sitting on the couch.

"Be careful around the glass Stacey," I say.

The kids are still cleaning.

"You want to watch TV?" Angeleek asks me.

"No," I say.

"You know time will fly and you'll be walking again in no time right?" Angeleek asks.

I say nothing and I'm trying not to breathe hard to let her know she's annoying as hell right now.

I'm crippled, angry and bitter.

"Maybe we can go sip a margarita or something when this is over," Angeleek continues.

It sounds like she wants to be friends but that can't happen. She done seen my cat and ass. I wouldn't feel right around her if we were friends.

"Angeleek, I'm not in the mood," I sya. "I'm about to go to sleep. You can change the sheets and blanket on my bed and use my room for the night."

Angeleek says alright and heads upstairs.

"Have Josiah give you the remoter," I say.

I throw up some of my water while Lanice puts more pictures of herself and the rest of my kids back on the shelf. She rushes to my side and kneels down.

"Mommy are you okay?" Lanice asks.

I throw up some more water.

"Angeleek!" I scream.

Angeleek and all my kids rush to the living room.

"I'm fine," I say breathing heavily. "Just leave me alone."

Lanice grabs a towel and cleans the water up. She's crying.

I close my eyes and try to go to sleep. I can't. I'm crying as I think of the good times me and my kids used to have.

My mind sharply transitions to the night I overhead them disrespecting me. Me giving them their punishment, and thought of the making arrangements to leave the house come to mind as well.

The day I heard the rapists come in, the sound of that think ass hail hitting my window, and each and every last one of those

bastards going in and out of me start to flash in my brain.

I open my eyes and Stacey is standing right in front of me.

"What?" I ask.

"Nothing," Stacey says.

"Go upstairs and have Angeleek come here," I say.

Chapter 41

I have Angeleek go to the store and get me some liquor.

After a couple shots I knock out. This will be my remedy until I can get past all the shit that happened.

I wake up the next day and the boys are gone.

The house is spick and span.

"Mom do you need to use the bathroom?" Lanice asks.

I shake my head no.

"I made you a chicken salad whenever you're hungry," Lanice says.

"What time is it?" I ask.

"Ten-thirty," Lanice says.

I don't know why I asked. I have no clue what time the boys left or what time practice is over.

I have Lanice go to my messages in my phone. I have over sixty-five. Everyone's worried about me.

I have Lanice send out a mass message saying I'm okay. I have her go to my *FriendSpot* account and type my name in the search bar just so I can see what everyone is saying. But for the most part everyone is wishing me well and praying for my recovery. I Some people are even giving testimonies about the crazy shit their kids did.

One woman says her son took her new car for a drive the day she got it and ran into a tree.

All I can think is at least her child only harmed himself. At least no one was gang banged and beat up.

There's some rape victims talking about how they overcame their abuse. Most are saying they went to therapy. I'm not doing that shit. Sitting down and telling somebody my business not gone happen. Plus, being that my story is all over the news and my kids have a lot of publicity, I can guarantee my damn nosy ass therapist would tell someone everything I said. Hell, I'm positive that for the right amount of money he or she would tell a

damn blog or news reporter.

People will do anything for a dollar.

I'm not going to therapy.

There's another woman saying her son was raped when he was four years old by a man. When her son got older he did the same thing to a four year old boy and now he's in prison.

Oh. There's a picture of me using my head and shoulder to hold my phone to talk.

This world is so fucked up. I have Lanice close the phone after that.

My boys walk in. They look ashamed and embarrassed as they sit on a card with some flowers on my table.

"Hi Mom," Josiah says.

For some reason all of my kids are being obedient. I don't want to say anything but I do need to talk to all they asses again.

"Both of you need to take a shower," I tell my boys. "When you're finished have everyone come down here and sit down."

"Yes ma'am," my boys says.

I have Alisa wheel me in front of the couches in front of everyone and ask Angeleek to go in my room.

Here I am once again trying to figure out how to start a conversation with my kids.

"How was practice?" I ask the boys.

"Okay," Josiah says.

"Do you guys love me?" I ask.

My kids either nod their heads or say yes.

"Look at me," I cry. "Just look. I wanted you guys to come save me so bad," I say looking at Josiah. "Do you think any of your teammates or friends would disrespect their parents like you guys did me? You didn't even bother to make sure nothing was recording Josiah?"

I'm still bitter behind that shit.

"I was disciplining you guys," I say.

I have a headache already. It's not even noon yet.

"Stacey give Mommy some of this water," I saylooking at my liquor bottle.

I needed that lil' swig.

"I guess what I need to get off my chest is this," I say. "I feel like I can't control you guys. And that's the one thing as a mother I need to feel like I have. Control. There's seven of you and I can't take a chance on that shit again. You guys have shown me that whenever you want to do something you will do it. No matter what I say. You pretty much told me that you will decide what punishment you deserve for your behavior. For fucking days you were gone. For fucking days I was being raped."

"We didn't know the weather would get bad," Alisa says. "We were going to come straight home after the game."

"After the game huh?" I rhetorically ask. "I know Grace was throwing you guys a party that night. You telling me you guys weren't going to go?"

They don't say anything.

"Which one of you opened my garage and didn't lock it?" I ask.

"I did," Alisa admits. "I thought we were taking our biked. I didn't know the boys called Mr. Wallace. I forgot."

"Well let's just try and make the best of our last two weeks together," I say. "There's not much I can do, but I guess we can talk about something."

"Can we just spend them with you Mom?" Josiah asks.

"No. I want you to play in the games," I say. "I meant what I said. If you're not going to play then I can call Mildred back and you guys can be on your way."

I have Josiah turn on the news and wheel me around towards the TV.

"Let's see what the worlds is saying about us now," I say.

After a few reports on killings, pictures of the men that raped me pop up on the screen. They're being charged with rape,

137

beating my ass, and burglary. Their sentences are still being decided.

How long could it possibly take for the judge to decide life?

The reporter goes on about how everything went down. She must've went down to the station and personally interviewed the cops because she's saying everything they said when they were here. She knows the boys are still practicing basketball so she's wondering if the rumor is true about me putting them in foster care.

A commercial comes on and I have Josiah turn the TV off.

"Mom anything. You just name it," Josiah says.

"What do you think you can do for me?" I ask. "What?! You don't want to go to Oxdale huh? Where every other week a child is saying they're being abused or runs away."

Oxdale is a group home for bad ass kids. They stay having problems. It's an hour drive away. It's not the closest one to me, but if I had my way I would send them there. These kids need to feel what I felt.

I tell them thanks for cleaning the house and send them to their rooms.

I nap all day.

For the next few days, my couch is my luxury. I only leave it when I need to use the bathroom. The kids stay on their best behavior.

I don't even use Angeleek anymore. I have the girls take me to the bathroom.

The girls were in the backyard and Angeleek was sleep one time so I had to have the boys take me. It was that time of the month, but they didn't show any sign of uncomfortableness. They naturally removed my pad and replaced it. They wiped me properly and returned me to my chair.

Before they walked away they asked me if I was feeling okay and if I needed anything else.

They're trying. But the ugly truth still remains. I was violated

by disgusting, low down ass men in the worst way possible.

My kids can never release me of that.

I have Mya come by and watch the kids the day Angeleek takes me to the hospital to get all my casts removed.

When I arrive home the kids smile at the sight of me. I try not to smile back, but it naturally comes out.

We have to hop on a flight to New York soon.

Chapter 42

We're packing for New York

I'm really trying not to lose the anger I had when I was being mistreated. The kids are all acting genuinely hurt about what happened to me. I'm forcing myself to think about my feelings when I realized they disobeyed me. Now I'm back to feeling a hundred percent sure that they're going to foster care.

I can't shake that shit.

"Boys, do you have everything ready for tomorrow?" I ask.

"Come in Mom," Justin says.

I don't.

"Everything's ready," Justin continues.

When we arrive to the airport, it's crowded as hell. I buy the kids something to eat and we wait with the rest of the team and parents on the plane to arrive.

Damn near every teenage girl that walks by smiles and tries to act like they the shit when they walk past my sons. They obviously don't give a fuck about the pain they caused me. However, my boy's teammates clearly do or they're putting on a front for me. The atmosphere is completely off. The team seems scared to even talk to my sons who have been on mute since we got to the terminal.

Bianca has to use the bathroom.

"Mom I don't got to go?" Stacey says.

"Try," I say.

When I get back from the restroom, Coach Eric asks to speak to me. He apologizes for everything that's happened.

"Don't worry about it," I say. "It's not your fault."

I let Bianca and Stacey stare out the window. When we take off, I make them go to sleep.

"Once you wake up we'll be there," I say.

We take a shuttle to the hotel that all the players and coaches are staying in. Me and my kids have two rooms. The ones that

have a door that connects them. This is perfect. Two beds is not enough for us.

Coach Eric is knocking at the door.

"Hi Ms. Leah. The boys need to stay with the team," Coach Eric says.

Josiah and Justin step out without their suitcases and talk to the coach. My head is on the door listening. Charise and Bianca can see me, but I don't care.

Josiah and Justin are explaining to Coach Eric that they really need to spend as much time with me as they can. They're saying they're working hard to rebuild our relationship before it's too late.

"Too late for what?" nosy ass Coach Eric asks.

"We just need to spend most of our time with her while we're here," Josiah says. "If we're not playing or shooting around we need to be with our mother."

"It's not right that I let you stay where you want and not the other boys," Coach Eric says.

"Then tell them we can't play," Josiah says.

Someone out there is knocking on the door now.

"He means that words can't explain how much our family is going through right now," Justin says. "We really need to comfort our mother. We gave you her number. Just call her phone if you need to."

Chapter 43

The boys have a late night shoot around.

Me and the girls eat dinner at a buffet, then we watch movies back in the room. When the boys finish practice they are more than happy to join us.

We fall asleep as soon as we get back in the room.

When I wake up, everyone else is knocked out. I wake my oldest three up and have them go in the other room.

"Mom can you sleep in here with us?" Justin asks.

I get in the bed with him.

"Mom do you forgive us yet?" Justin asks.

"I don't want to talk Justin. I just want to go to sleep," I say.

Chapter 44

The boys win the first game of their tournament.

A lot of people keep glancing over at me and the girls. People are looking at me, whispering and shit.

Anyways.

The boys play a second game late in the evening and win.

Back at the hotel we play a few board games, as a family, that the kids brought from the house.

There is one time I actually genuinely laugh and that's when Bianca hits her pinky toe on the side of the bed.

I feel the love from my kids for a while when we talk and play the games, but it instantly goes away when I get to remembering.

They used to show me affection all the time before I overheard how they really felt about me.

I'm ready to go to bed, but Bianca and Stacey still need a bath.

I have Alisa do it.

Josiah gives me a hug and makes sure his head touches my forehead.

Chapter 45

The championship game rolls around and everyone in the crowd is on their feet the entire time.

Jump ball goes up and the crowd gets loud. This looks like a fucking track meet mixed with basketball. Some of these players are really, really fast.

The half-time show is free throw shooting contests for gift cards.

People keep glancing back an forth at me and my girls. I wish the damn parents would at least stop looking at me and talking to their neighbor or on the phone.

Half-time concludes and the teams run back out.

I see Justin, but Josiah is nowhere to be found. Neither is the assistant coach. I go to the locker room and see my son sitting with his head in his lap. The assistant coach is upset.

"I don't understand why you would do this now," the assistant coach says. "You've come way too far."

"Let me talk to my son," I sternly say to this bastard ass assistant coach.

The assistant coach leaves out.

"Mom I'm sorry," Josiah cries. "I'm sorry I let you down. I can't live without you. Please don't give us away."

"Josiah," I say. "I want you to get back on the court and win this game. I'm going to be more upset if I went through all that shit so you could set your team up to make it here, and you don't even get what you bargained for. This is what you wanted right? This is why I was raped? This is why our family name is even more tarnished and I'm dealing with all types of bitches out there staring at me and whispering to they friends. And don't worry. It's not because of my eyebrows."

Josiah's crying ass kisses my cheek.

"You're beautiful Mom," Josiah says. "It was a bad night."

I don't care about shit any of my kids say concerning that

night. If they weren't caught, they'd probably still be having club meetings talking bad about me and making jokes about my eyebrows.

"Josiah," I say. "Right now, I want you to prove to me that you can be obedient and get back out there on the court. Your team doesn't deserve this. Give me a hug son."

He hugs me tightly with his forehead pressing hard against my neck. I can't trust him, but for right now I need to tell him what he needs to hear. He can never gain back the spot he once had in my heard. I lead the way to the bathroom here in the locker room so I can wipe his face of his tears.

"I love you Mom," Josiah says.

"I love you too Son," I say. "Go out there and win this game for me. Can you do that for me?"

Josiah nods his head.

He joins his team on the bench. He's on the end. The coaches and team are pissed at his ass. When I look at the score, I know why. We're only up ten with a minute left in the third quarter.

"Mommy is Josiah okay?" Stacey asks.

"Yea. He's fine," I say.

What the hell is going on? We're only up a little. Coach Eric is fussing. This is unheard of when it comes to us.

Josiah turns around on the bench and looks up at me.

I wink at him.

Now we're in the fourth quarter, without the lead. The opponent's fans are going crazy.

Coach Eric calls a timeout. Josiah's checking in.

One of the opponent's players is whispering something in Justin's ear. Justin punches the hell out of him. The referee is trying to pull Justin back, but Justin wont' stop punching. He is stomping on the boy's face and kicking him until he no longer can now. Both boys are ejected from the game.

Josiah better put more than his all in the rest of this game now that Justin's ejected. He better remember this game means I

145

didn't get abused for nothing.

Josiah hist a three and the other team calls a timeout.

Josiah looks up at me again and I wink at him.

We now have less than a minute in the game. Josiah steals the ball. He pulls up for the three and knocks it down. The whole building explodes.

Thirty seconds left. The other team quickly launches the ball down court and makes a lay-up.

Coach Eric calls his last timeout.

Back on the court, Josiah throws the ball at the other team's basket.

"Josiah!" I yell.

I should've never told his ass that he loved basketball more than me. At least not until after this damn game.

Josiah's walking off the court. Two of his teammates on the bench attack him. They punch him in the chest repeatedly. This raggedy bastard, Coach Eric, takes his sweet precious time to get to my son. He wants these boys to fuck him up.

I rush down to help Josiah. The damn referees get to him before his fucking coach did and the coach was the closest. I walk with the referees as they escort Josiah to the locker room.

"I can handle it from here," I tell the referees.

I close the locker room door. Josiah sits next to his brother.

Before I say a word, the crowd erupts. I can't make out what everyone is chanting.

"I love you more than this fucking game," Josiah says.

"Get your stuff," I say. "We need to go before them boys get in here."

My boys don't move.

"Josiah and Justin get your stuff," I say.

They still don't move.

"Okay," I say. "So what you're telling me is you still gone do what you want?"

"Can I explain to the team the mistake I made?" Josiah asks.

146

"Josiah," I say. "Believe me. You don't want to make any fresher what just happened on that court in their minds, and I don't want to see anybody else get into it. Not here."

"I want to tell them I made a mistake not listening to you," Josiah says. "I want to go out there in front of the cameras and apologize for the pain we caused you."

It's only a matter of time before some angry boys walk in. And fuck. The girls are still out there.

"Listen to me," I say. "If you want to apologize publicly, I can set something up. It's nothing for me to hit up Eva and give her an interview. Everybody is waiting to hear the story from our lips."

Wait. They already have technically.

"Let's talk when we get back to California," I say. "Right now I just want you two to prove to me you can obey me and get your stuff so we can go please."

They grab everything and wait for me outside while I go get the girls.

Judging by the overly happy opponents fans talking on their cell phones, and the score board, we just lost.

I hope this shuttle hurries the fuck up.

Chapter 46

"I want to tank you girls for behaving while I was in the locker room," I say.

We're on a shuttle back to the airport. The tickets are for tomorrow, but I'm paying to switch them. We're not safe if we stay.

The entire flight back I'm contemplating on what I want to do. A part of me doesn't want to let them go to foster care. What if they get with a good family that makes them happy? What if they just stop caring about me? I like that they're sucking up to me. I want them to keep doing it. I don't want them to do well at anything. I want to make them really understand what I went through.

I need to make them do something that no one wants to do and will scar them for the rest of their lives like I am. Me guaranteeing a lifetime of pain will make me feel a whole lot better than putting them in a system where they may or may not get treated the way I'm hoping they do, which is bad.

My kids are gorgeous and have talent. Somebody will adopt them quick because they will make a lot of money.

I'm going to hold off on the foster care notion. My mind is fucked and I want to make sure I fuck up theirs too. I need to figure something out, but in the meantime, I'm just going to schedule an interview with Eva.

The next morning Stacey and Bianca are playing with toys. I know their siblings are pretending to be sleep. I'm not gone say nothing though. I'm just gone see how long they play me for a fool. I make the girls cereal for breakfast.

"You guys ready to start back school?" I ask. Bianca and Stacey.

They both say yes, and shake their heads no. I laugh and ask why they don't want to go.

"School's too hard," Stacey says. "It's too much trying to

148

read."

"Well you gone have to learn how to read if you trying to sing and act," I say. "Mommy don't want to keep reading everything."

I send *The Eva Show* an email stating she can have the first interview.

We're due for an appearance in a few days.

I alert the boys of the news. They're relieved that I'm not getting rid of them today. I'm not getting rid of them period, but they don't know that yet. They'll probably wish I did when I figure out what I'm gone do.

I sit on the bed with Justin and brief the kids on how Ms. Eva gets down with her talk show.

"She likes to get the nitty gritty," I say. "She's gone get as personal as she can. If you get emotional, fight that shit because she's not gone care."

Ms. Eva is nosy. She's straight cut-throat. She has the highest rated talk show in America and her show is gone skyrocket even more when me and the kids explain all the fuckery that's happened.

"I'm ready Mama," Josiah says. "I don't want anyone thinking you did anything to deserve what we said and did."

"I'm ready too Mom," Justin says. "This will be the only time I have to apologize for anything like this because it won't happen again."

"So make sure you have everything you want to say ready and be prepared to tell what part you played in the shit that happened to me," I say. "My arm is bothering me," I lie. "I need to take a nap."

Truth is, I just want some peace and quiet in my room.

Chapter 47

I dress business casual for *The Eva Show*. I know it must've
killed Charise to put on a pair of pants and shirt that I picked out.

We arrive to the show and are escorted by a lady to a huge
lounging room. There's fruits and veggies with dip, bottled
water, and cut up sandwiches on a long table with flowers and
balloons. There's also a flat screen TV that shows the stage we'll
be on.

People are out there setting up chairs and playing around with
camera focus. Me and the kids sit down on this nice couch.

"She wants to interview you guys in groups," the escort says.
She reads for a paper. "First Lanice and Charise. Then Bianca
and Stacey. Then the last three. Then Mom. Then everyone
together."

"Okay," I say.

The escort shuts the door behind her.

"You guys nervous?" I ask the kids.

"No," Justin says.

He's ready to hop his ass on the microphone and talk to the
world.

I can't wait to hear what these kids have to say. I only have
one regret and that's not predicting some questions and
practicing answering them while I was at home.

Ms. Eva comes in the room.

"Hello Ms. Leah," Ms. Eva says. "How are you?"

"Fine," I say.

This lady is not fooling me. She's all cool now, but I know
once we on that stage she gone turn into a nosy bitch that can't
stop being so damn nosy. I don't understand how someone can
spend most of their lives asking people a bunch of damn
questions. And about the issues they have in their house. It's like
this woman catches an orgasm from asking people that shit she
knows they don't want to answer. She should've called this damn

show *Question Mark.*

"Let me take you guys to hair and makeup," Ms. Eva says.

One difference between Ms. Eva and us is we don't need makeup. She wears a lot to cover up her wrinkles and what I see now are huge bags under her eyes.

Me and the kids follow her to a very nice vanity room where there's people waiting to dazzle us up.

"Mommy do you want us to put on makeup?" Stacey asks.

"No I don't," I say. "Please just do their hair," I say to all the hair and makeup people.

"You want an up-do or your hair down?" one hair stylist asks me.

"Down," I say.

Chapter 48

The escort comes for Lanice and Charise. Me and the rest of my kids watch the show on the screen in the lounge.

"Now let's cut to the chasse," Ms. Eva says.

She's not wasting no time. Her nosy ass is just pure fucking eager to get the facts. Like damn anything good, let's just talk about the bad. No how you doing or nothing. Wait. I guess she did ask that backstage.

"You and your siblings snuck out the house, went to the state championship, and got stranded with the Wallace family due to the weather for a few days. True or false?" Ms. Eva asks.

The hell is this? A lie detector test. I can't stand people like her. So damn eager to hear negative shit. This woman is off to me.

"Yes," Lanice and Charise say.

"During those days your mother was raped repeatedly by multiple men," Ms. Eva says. "What were you guys thoughts when you heard the news about your mother and what were you doing?"

Charise says they all broke down. They're hearts were broken and they couldn't believe what happened.

"We were at the Wallace's," Lanice says. "The weather got too bad so Mr. Ron wanted to get off the road and took us to his house."

The girls tell Ms. Eva the only thing they were expecting to happen was for a harsher punishment when they got home.

"right. You guys were supposed to make it home the same day of the game but the weather prevented that?" Ms. Eva asks.

The girls nod their heads.

"Do you guys have any regrets?" Ms. Eva asks.

The girls say yes.

"Knowing what you know now, would you have still left the house?" Ms. Eva asks.

Lanice and Charise say no.

Lanice also says it's the worst mistake they ever made.

"Was it really a mistake if you premeditated to do it?" Ms. Eva asks. "You planned to leave the house. You knew what you were doing was wrong. You just didn't know that one little small action could have a tremendous consequence."

Lanice says, "We're very ashamed, disappointed, and embarrassed at what they did to our mother."

"We don't want people thinking that we don't love our mother because we do," Charise says. "We just made a bad decision and we'll make it up to her the rest of our lives if we have to."

"Who took it the hardest?" Ms. Eva asks.

"As soon as Josiah heard what hospital our mother was at, he ran out the house," Charise says. "He only made it a block before he fell to his knees and broke down. Mr. Ron and his oldest daughter had to help him get back inside."

"I assume he was running to the hospital," Ms. Eva says.

The girls nod their heads.

"Did Ron know your brothers weren't supposed to play in the game?" Ms. Eva asks. "Why didn't he get a confirmation from Leah?" When did you guys tell him the entire truth about what was going on? What was his reaction?"

"He didn't know they weren't supposed to play," Charise answers. "He trusted that we would never lie to him. Lanice told him everything when the news said she was dead."

"You guys thought your mother was dead?" Ms. Eva asks.

"Yes," Charise says. "The news said she dies shortly after getting to the hospital."

"When did you find out she was still alive?" Ms. Eva asks.

"Josiah was about to stab himself, but Mr. Ron got the knife out his hands before he could and held him tight," Lanice says. "That's when his oldest daughter let us know Mom wasn't dead."

"And that's when Josiah ran out the house?" Ms. Eva asks.

"Yes," both Lanice and Charise say.

Ms. Eva takes a commercial break.

Chapter 49

Bianca and Stacey take a seat on the stage.

Me and Ms. Eva both learn that they asked Mr. Ron if they could live with him when they thought I was dead because they didn't want to live with their dad.

They say Mr. Ron didn't give them an answer.

Ms. Eva asks the girls if they will ever disobey me again and they say no.

Pretty much my kids follow behind one another. If one doesn't like someone, none of them do.

Chapter 50

My oldest three take the stage.

"Were you guys worried at all about your mother before you found out she was being abused?" Ms. Eva asks.

"No," Justin admits. "Just really worried about how much worse our restrictions would be."

"I wasn't worried at first," Alisa says. "But once I remembered we took her phone I was. We're very sorry and remorseful for what we caused our mom. The boys worked so hard all season and we didn't want them to have done it for nothing."

"You guys didn't want them to have done it for nothing?" Ms. Eva repeats. "So why did you throw the ball to the other teams basket Josiah?"

"My mother thinks we love basketball more than her, and I wanted to show her we didn't," Josiah says. "She is my heart."

"What did the other play say to you that med you snap?" Ms. Eva asks looking at Justin.

"He kept throwing it in my face that it was our fault what happened to my mom," Justin says. "He said gang-banged and it hit my heart really hard."

"So the men that harmed your mother are still awaiting sentences. How do you guys feel about that?" Ms. Eva asks.

"Like that process is taking too long," Josiah says. "They should be getting life or the chair."

"Who came up with the idea to just leave?" Ms. Eva asks. "Who was the mastermind?"

"Justin joked about the idea, Charise said we should do it, and then we all just figured out how we would go," Alisa reveals.

"Was it worth it?" Ms. Eva asks.

"No," Josiah says.

Chapter 51

I meet Mildred and Tiffany in the lobby. I'm gone try and heal on my own. These last few days with the kids have been pure hell. They were painful to look at. Every time I looked at one of them, or they called me mom, my heart felt the same anger it did when I found out they left and made sure I was stranded.

I honestly couldn't think of anything I could do to them that would make me feel better and not get a jail or prison sentence if they snitched. Besides. This is the right thing to do. I'm a good woman. Ain't no child gone take that away from me.

"Thanks for coming," I say to the two ladies. "We should be done in another hour."

"You're up next," the escort says to me. "Are these your friends?"

"No," I say. "They're the foster care people. Can you put them in a separate room? I don't want the kids to know they're here yet."

"Sure," the escort says. "Just let me take you to the stage."

"I know how to get there," I say. "I need to check on my kids."

My youngest four are sitting tight. I tune back into the TV.

"I'll do anything to make my mom feel better," Josiah says. "I don't care if she tosses me in a room with a bunch of evil people. As long as she can get back to loving me like she used to, then I don't care what I have to live with. If she needs me to feel what she felt, I will."

Ms. Eva does my introduction.

"Our next guest is the mother of all the kids you just saw on the stage," Ms. Eva says. "She's been to hell and back and she's here with us today to share her story. Ladies and gentlemen, please put your hands together for Leah Rogers."

My boys and Alisa try to hug me and I move back. No love needs to be transferred anymore.

157

I get a nice applause as I take my seat.

"Let me start by saying thank you for joining us today," Ms. Eva says. "I know it's not easy sharing a tough experience. I was surprised I even got an email from you."

Little does she know it's not about sharing the experience. It's about exposing these bastards I have to call kids. What better way is there to let the world know how bad my stupid, self-centered and sneaky seven are, than them admitting it themselves?

"It's no problem," I lie.

"Why don't' you share with us what happened, starting with finding out your kids snuck out the house," Ms. Eva says. "I just couldn't imagine what I would do if I had children and my little ones weren't there when I woke up. Tell us what was going through your mind and your initial reaction when you found out they weren't there. First off, how did you learn that they went to the game?"

Ms. Eva's nosy ass just can't get her antsy mind on what nosy ass questions she wants to ask first.

"I found out from the TV," I say.

I always wanted to do this show but not for some bullshit. I was expecting to sit with her and discuss my kid's careers and upcoming projects. I wanted her to talk about all our success. But here I am admitting to this woman bad shit that's happened to me. I can barely talk and this bitch doesn't care. She just wants answers. It's like she's enjoying me talk through my pain. I can barely open my mouth. She's starting to seem sick to me. She's lucky she's paying me a hefty amount to do this shit. I don't like talking about anything negative period.

"When you were in the house being abused for all those days, were you concerned about your kids?" Ms. Eva asks.

"I was a little," I say.

"A little?" Ms. Eva asks.

"Yes. A little," I say. "I was mainly worried about my

youngest two. The oldest ones I hold responsible for what happened to me, so I honestly wouldn't have cared if anything happened to them. It would've been their fault. They were supposed to be home with me."

"When you say you wouldn't have cared about what happened to them, do you mean like being hurt or being killed?" Ms. Eva asks.

"Both," I say.

I hate when her proper ass repeats the phrases I say that aren't correct English. I don't like how she repeated *wouldn't have cared*.

"Why did you let them still play in nationals?" Ms. Eva asks.

"Because I didn't want everything that's happened to me to have been for nothing," I say.

"What did you think of the outcome of the game?" Ms. Eva asks.

"I was disappointed," I say. "I definitely wanted them to win first place after everything that happened."

"Your sons said you think they love basketball more than you," Ms. Eva says.

I nod my head.

"Let me ask you this," Ms. Eva says. "Let's say you weren't raped, never burglarized and the kids made it home that same day. Would you feel that way?"

"Yes," I say. "Their little video that's spreading like wildfire across the internet tells me they don't love me at all."

We go to commercial break.

Chapter 52

Ms. Eva has all of my kids come on stage with me.

She tells the audiences how all the kids can sing, dance and act and how good the boys are in basketball.

"Everyone saw this family as the complete package," Ms. Eva says. "Talented beyond belief and good looking. There's not much more a parent could ask for."

"There certainly is," I correct her. "A kind heart is very important. Especially when it comes to your mother."

"I mean, I assumed they had good hearts along with the talent and looks," Ms. Eva says.

I know she one of them bitches that only care about the damn dollar.

"A lot of parents have issues with their children, but many don't have repercussions like you did when it comes to their behavior," Ms. Eva says. "Let's talk about the video that made you take away their privilege in the first place. Let's start with you Charise. It's clear in the video that you're upset at the stares your mother gets and are embarrassed to be around her at times. That shocks me because of all the footage and pictures I've seen of you and her together, I don't get that you're uncomfortable or embarrassed by her. You actually have a lot of pictures on the internet with her and they only give off love. Josiah as well. Tell us why you said those things."

"The truth," I angrily say.

"It was on one of my favorite singer's pages and I saw that he posted a picture of me and Lanice with eyebrows like you," Charise says. "A lot of people said they were laughing in the comments and the post had thousands of likes and comments. People do it all the time and I just got sick of it. A lot of famous people make jokes about you. I just had an off night and started running my mouth."

I'm shedding tears now. Not only are people making it hard

160

for me, they're making it hard for my kids. I knew about the postings, I just didn't know my kids were hiding that they were bothered by them.

I now know that my kids were acting unbothered because they didn't want the world to see that they were ashamed of their mother's eyebrows.

"So pretty much you're upset at me because I wasn't created with cute eyebrows?" I ask.

"No," Charise cries.

"You hate me because there are cruel people in the world that give people that are born different a hard time?" I ask. "Are you the one spreading pictures around of me with nicer looking eyebrows too?"

I wish people would just stare at home through the computer screen. These days they want me to see the evil looks to make my heart heavy. I know it's to enhance their sex.

"No. That isn't me Mommy," Charise says. "I don't hate you."

I don't believe her.

"You know I'm happy that none of my kids came out with eyebrows like mine," I say. "Just because of this very reason right here. I never wanted my kids to have to deal with anything I've dealt with that was negative. I have to deal with every day issues on top of my eyebrows which makes life harder for me."

"I'm sorry Mom," Charise says. "We didn't mean it. We just had a bad night. We all love you and don't want to hurt you. You're the only mother we want. No one can replace you."

"Would you be sorry if you weren't caught?" Ms. Eva asks.

"Yes," Charise says. "It was just a stupid night and I got overwhelmed."

"Do you guys all agree that it was a bad night?" Ms. Eva asks.

The kids all say yes.

"We love our mom and we apologize for what we said, not

obeying her and everything that's happened to her," Josiah says. "If we could take it back we would."

"Are you guys embarrassed by your mother?" Ms. Eva asks. They all say no.

"What's your relationship with your kids now?" Ms. Eva asks me.

"It's definitely not what it used to be," I say. "Sometimes I don't' want to look at them or hear their voices."

"Leah do you think your family is ruined?" Ms. Eva asks me.

"It's something I don't think about," I say. "I'm just trying to move forward. But if you're referring to a celebrity stand point, meaning their money will go down, then maybe it will affect them negatively in a small way but not a big one. It's not like they sent them damn criminals to my house."

Wait. I can't trust these bastards for shit.

"You guys didn't send them to my damn house did you?!" I ask.

"Why would we do that!?" Josiah asks. "You are our mother! We're sorry for leaving you! We're sorry for all the shit that's happened!"

"Leah, where was your phone?" Ms. Eva asks.

"I just knew I left it in the room with me," I say.

"I took the phone," Alisa admits. "Justin slashed one of the car tires and I made sure to take her car keys."

"What do you guys want to say to your mother and let the world know before we conclude?" Ms. Eva asks.

"Mom I love you and I'm so proud to be your son," Josiah says. "I hate myself for not listening to you. I want you to be happy and have a good life. I want to protect you. I'm sorry I let you down as your oldest. I promise I won't disappoint you again."

Josiah gets up to give me a kiss and sits back down.

"Will you be able to get past this?" Ms. Eva asks me.

"Right now, no," I say. "But I will be if you allow my tow

guests to come out."

Mildred and Tiffany come on stage. The kids are now in tears. Charise runs backstage.

"Who are they?" Ms. Eva asks.

"Foster care," I say.

Ms. Eva is not happy.

"You know one of the things I've always admired about you is the fact that at such a young age you are able to take care of yourself and kids," Ms. Eva lowly says. "Not a lot of people could pull off what you have."

I guess foster care is the best way for me to get back at these kids and all the ugly bastards that ever laughed at anything they said bad about me.

"I heard the rumors, but I definitely didn't think they were true," Ms. Eva says. "Have you been planning all along to put them in foster care?"

"I've been battling back and forth with the idea," I say. "Once I realized that I wasn't getting better because I had the people responsible for hurting me in my face every day, I knew I had to make a change. Maybe Vayda will adopt you Charise. I know you'll love that. She's beautiful, has a great career, she's dumb as fuck and loves to hit her child, but I'm sure you don't care. I'm sure she's watching now. Y'all can sip tea and do each other's hair while y'all chat all day about being pretty."

Ms. Eva sends the show to a commercial break.

Chapter 53

Alisa and Lanice are squeezing me tight and crying their hearts out.

"It's time for you guys to go," I say.

They don't let go.

Ms. Eva is not saying nothing and that's good because it's not her place to tell me what to do with my kids. She can't relate to shit that's happened to me. I know she was reaped, but that was by one person. She doesn't know what the fuck I'm going through. She doesn't even have kids. She thinks I'm fucking stupid too. I can clearly see the red lights still on the cameras.

Ms. Eva is still recording us.

"Please don't do this Mom," Josiah says.

"Charise locked herself in the bathroom stall," the escort says. I don't care.

I'm trying to push Alisa and Lanice off me but they have such a good grip. I'm trying to elbow them. I'm pissed as all hell that the studio workers aren't helping me. There's also security guards that can make their muscular asses my way. The girls hold on as long as they can. I'm pinching them.

"You guys did this shit!" I yell.

"We're sorry," Alisa cries. "It was one mistake."

One mistake? Every little thing this girl says wrong pisses me off. They talked shit about me, created fucking hateful ass accounts about me, and snuck out the house which is why the robbers thought no one was home.

"Get the hell out of here," I demand.

Now Josiah and Justin have their arms wrapped around me. This is too fucking much.

"I love you Mom," Josiah cries. "I'll do anything. Don't separate our family. This is our fault. We'll fix it."

This shit is fucking embarrassing. I know the people at home that are watching live feel like they're watching a soap opera.

This shit is unbelievable.

Giving up on these boys letting me go, I finally say, "Alright! Have a seat!"

The boys slowly let me go. We're all sitting back down. I'm staring at Ms. Eva waiting for her to say something because I sure as hell don't know what I want to say. I just want these kids gone.

"Is there anything we can do here, to make you reconsider your decision?" Ms. Eva asks. "I think you're making a terrible mistake."

I'm at a loss for words. And now I look like a heartless bitch because I'm laughing. I can't take this shit serious no more. They did this. These dumb ass kids can't accept their consequences.

"What if I paid for a vacation for you and your kids?" Ms. Eva asks. "Roundtrip. Everything's on me. Anywhere you want to go for two weeks."

I want these kids to take me serious and regret what they did for the rest of their lives. I want them to feel guilty every single time they take a breath. They're not going to feel my pain so the least I can do is make them live without their mother and walk around feeling ashamed that it's no one's fault but their own.

I think Ms. Eva is worried the kids will be separated and put with bad parents. She needs to think about what happened to me, and what happened to me only.

However, Ms. Eva just made a good offer.

"I'll rent out a house for you and your children," Ms. Eva says. "I'll even pay for a few shopping sprees. I just don't want you to act off of your feelings right now."

I feel like I'm not gone get out of here unless I have a change of heart.

"Alright fine. Hawaii," I say.

I'm just trying to get a free vacation.

The escort brings Charise back on the stage.

"I want to thank you guys for coming out," Ms. Eva says. "I

think you're a strong woman. Myself as well as the rest of the world are going for your family. I do think what happened is awful, but I also think with time your family can get back to what it was before any of this happened. Your empire can still be built. Don't give up on them yet."

Chapter 54

Alisa and Josiah come with me to make groceries. Someone bumps into me walking down the aisle and Josiah pushes him and they start fighting.

Two male workers have to separate the boys. Now I have someone trailing us around to make sure Josiah doesn't do nothing else. He needs to calm his ass down.

I release Mya when I get to the house and make the kids red beans and rice with pig tails. I'm only doing it because I'm tired of sandwiches and noodles. They eat at the dining room table. I eat in the living room and watch *Just Shine.*

Shit. I didn't buy no damn alcohol.

"I'm about to go to the store and get us something to drink," I say.

"We can drink water Momma if you don't feel like going," Josiah says.

"It's fine. I need you to look after them," I say. I don't care if they're home alone at the moment.

When I get back, Alisa comes and checks on me in my room.

"Can I do anything for you Mom?" Alisa asks.

When I finish eating, I have her take my plate.

Josiah does it. I make him take his clothes off next. He strips down with no problem. They know their momma is retaliating.

"Go inside your sister Josiah," I say.

I keep drinking. I'm in my right mind though. Josiah's putting his penis inside Alisa.

"Go in her fast," I say.

I want him to break her shit with no mercy. That'll give her ass some good pain. Josiah forces his shit in her fast as fuck. Her face is pained. She's still a virgin like she better be.

"Keep going until you finish," I say.

It takes Josiah too long to finish. He's not no damn virgin. Now I want to know if Justin's a virgin.

Justin goes inside Alisa and takes a few minutes to cum too.

He's not a virgin.

The boys probably lost their virginity to Grace.

Whatever.

I make Justin and Josiah stare at Alisa's face.

"You feel all that shit dripping out of you?" I ask. "Do you? I had five people's cum dripping out of me. Imagine a bunch of strangers putting that shit inside you. Licking all over you. Don't try. At least you know your damn brothers are clean. I'm lucky as fuck I don't have no damn diseases."

I'm pacing the room sipping my bottle.

"Go clean yourselves up," I say. I stop Josiah. "You'll do anything right?"

Josiah looks me directly in my eyes and whispers, "Yes."

Chapter 56

I go to sleep with a headache and the phone call I receive in the morning makes things worse.

A lady that works for some deformities and disabilities cause wants me to speak in front of her students. My minds is made up that I'm not doing that shit because I know why she wants me, but I want to see if she will say it, so I ask, "Why?"

"You're so beautiful and you've inspired so many people with your success and raising your kids," the lady says.

I know she's bullshitting me.

"I'm going to ask you again," I say. "Why? And don't lie because I'll know, and that will be the reason I say no."

"We think so many people admire you because of how you embrace your eyebrows," the lady says.

I hang up before she says another thing. She's not about to use me to help people with deformities. Fuck that bitch for making me even think about having eyebrows that are too bushy. I never looked at myself that way until her ugly ass put it in my head.

I'm furious.

I don't want any damn reminders that I have bushy eyebrows. I already have to look in the mirror every damn day. I don't want to be around people that have bodily issues. I don't want to be around people I will look at and instantly start thinking about my eyebrows. I just don't. At least not these days when I'm angry.

Fuck that bitch and her program or whatever it is. I'm pissed off but I'm glad she asked me over the phone instead of putting me in a position where it would be hard to say no which is in front of a group of people.

Chapter 57

Me and the kids are in my bathroom.

I take a few shots of liquor. I'm still well aware of what I'm doing.

I duct tape my kid's hands together and hit them all repeatedly on their asses. They're all working hard to scream as loud as they can.

I'm tired as hell. After a few minutes of enjoying them suffer, I cut the tape off and make them take a shot out my bottle.

"Go to your rooms, get yourselves together and come back," I say.

The doorbell rings.

"It's Grace," Justin says looking out the window.

This girl is on my nerves. It wasn't that long ago that I said I would put them in foster care and she already thinks they can have company.

"What do you want lil' girl?" I ask.

"Can I talk to Justin for a minute?" Grace asks.

"Grace, Justin is punished," I say. "He's not gone have no company for a while. Sorry. But when they can talk, I'll cut their phones back on."

Her fast ass probably just misses his dick. I go back in my bathroom. I'm laughing looking at these pathetic ass kids.

"You guys look awful," I say. "What happened? Get out my face and shut my room door when you leave."

I lean my back up against the door, sink down and cry.

Why did this shit have to happen? Why did the weather have to fuck up those particular days? What's wrong with those kids to leave me without any communication? Why did I have to have these fucking eyebrows? Just why? I'm pitying myself and losing my strength.

When I was a kid, I was not as heartless as the ones I have. I had a female friend that was completely bald on most of her

head. I had another friend that had a huge birthmark on her leg.

I was a good person.

There's no excuse for my sorry ass kids to have said that shit about me. I'm more upset at the things they said about me than being raped. But the thing I'm most angry about is being crippled for so damn long and needing people to help me do every damn thing.

If these kids want to remain in this fucking house, then they gone put up with any and everything I want them to.

I call the cable company and turn it off. I can't deal with no ore stories about us.

I just can't.

All the publicity was cool until it turned bad. I'm fucking done. No cable and no fucking internet. I cut all that shit off. The kids don't need to do nothing but eat, sleep and do whatever the hell I tell them to.

I have my oldest three strip in my cold ass garage, and I play games on my phone while they stand in the same spot. After a few hours I have them put their clothes back on and meet me in my room. I spray air freshener to give the illusion that I just shitted.

I put a bandana over Josiah's eyes and have him reach in the toilet. He pulls out banana slices and eats them. I have Justin do the same.

"Please don't Mom," Alisa says. "I'll do anything else."

"Girl put the shit in your mouth," I say.

She feels the banana and throws up. I take the bandana off her head.

"Clean this shit up and get the fuck out my room," I say.

Chapter 58

I dazzle up and prepare to be honored for my writing at *The Star Writer's Awards* show. The host wanted my kids to present to me but I told her that would ruin my night. So I ended up hiring seven kid actors, who are either Hispanic or Caucasian, to come with me.

"Where are your kids?" the host Helen asks.

"Right here," I say.

Helen takes me to a private room and shuts the door.

"Leah. Don't do this," Helen says. "Why wouldn't you want your real kids here for tonight?"

"They're on punishment," I say. "And you heard what they said right? They're embarrassed by me. They don't like my eyebrows. I'm doing them a favor by not making them come."

My real kids are at Mya's house. I hope they hate themselves right now.

"You're about to be the first black woman to get this award and you don't want your kids here to present to you?" Helen asks.

"I don't. If they're here, I'll think everyone that's laughing and smiling are doing so because of what they said and did to me," I say. "I won't enjoy a second of this night. I worked too hard to be miserable on a night like this because of my cold-blooded ass kids."

"You're being petty Leah," Helen says. "They're kids. They're going to make mistakes."

Here she goes with this shit I don't want to hear. I hate when people blame people's actions on their age. It's not about age. It's either they know better or they don't. My kids have a good mother.

It's the good parents that get the worst kids and the bad parents that get the good ones.

"Hell, I'm sure my kids say shit about me behind my back

too," Helen says. "I'm not gone hold no grudge on them. I'm gone beat they ass or punish them for a week. Maybe even increase their chores. But I wouldn't have them at home on a night like this. Definitely not if they're sorry."

I hate when people assume others are sorry.

"They've permanently scarred me," I say.

"Girl, no one is checking for that video no more," Helen says. "The shows about to start. You're not going on until later. You still have time to go get your real kids here."

"No," I say. "I already paid these kids."

When it's almost time for me to take the stage, Helen briefs the audience about me inspiring other's to bring some of their stories to life, my seminars, my background, and the success of my books, with the seven kids I brought with me. Helen even speaks about me being able to care for seven kids on my own.

"Ladies and gentlemen, please put your hands together for the one and only Leah Rogers," one of the boys I brought with me says.

I wave and blow a kids to the cameras. One of the girls I brought with me hands me my trophy and another one hands me a plaque.

I begin my speech.

"I want to start off my thanking God for another day. I'd like to thank my editors for helping me make my stories the best they could be. I'd like to thank the publishing companies for having faith in my stories. Most importantly, I'd like to thank all my supporters out there. Without you I'm not up here right now. I'd also like to thank these beautiful kind-hearted kids for presenting to me."

I purposely don't thank my real kids. Fuck they asses.

After the show, I meet my presenters at a nice buffet. Cameras follow me all the way to the restaurant.

I love it.

I can't wait for my real kids to see all the stuff I'm doing

without them. I don't need them to have a good time.

I'm surprised they didn't try to runaway to the police station when I wasn't around. They really must want to deal with their evil momma as a way to show they're sincerely sorry. They must think I deserve to get revenge.

And I do.

And I'm going to keep getting it until I feel better.

Chapter 59

I attend a photo-shoot for successful writers and entrepreneurs. After the photos, we're all interviewed separately.

"I love writing because I love to tell stories," I say. "In all of my stories I like people to get some kind of message. It's a way to teach people that you don't know, things you want them to learn. It's a way to say things you don't want to say because you know people will get offended by it. Nothing really inspired me to write. I've just always loved doing it."

Every one eats together after the photos and interviews.

I feel weird realizing that there's every day people that walk around smiling, laughing and pretending like life is all good, then they go home and beat the hell out of somebody, and I'm one of them. These women have no clue that a child abuser is amongst them. All they know is I was abused for days. They feel sympathy for me. It's never going to cross their mind that I have a single evil bone in my body.

When I get home, I send my youngest four to Mya's house to spend the night. Alisa, Josiah and Justin stay with me.

I advise them to put on some comfortable clothes.

"Move the couches to the wall," I say.

It's fight night. I make Josiah and Justin beat the shit out of each other.

"Do more," I say. "I want to feel like I'm watching a boxing match."

There's lots of elbowing and chokeholds.

Alisa is crying. "Suck it up," I say.

I have the boys take a break and they both fall to the floor. Justin is crying. Josiah looks angry. They both are sweating.

"Justin, get your crying ass up," I say. "How much crying you think I did when you were in that room laughing at me? When I was being raped by those men? Some of my fucking bones broke!" I yell. "And you crying over your fucking brother? Oh

what? You mad because you lost? Punch Alisa in the stomach and you better do it good."

"Just do it," Alisa cries.

Justin punches her.

"Okay. We're done for the night," I say.

Josiah apologizes to Justin when they walk to their room. Justin tells him to shut up. Josiah definitely beat his ass.

Wait. They're fighting again in their room. I sit down and watch.

Justin is crying hard. Josiah beat him again.

Justin is a sore loser.

After the second fight, I create a second *FriendSpot* account. I create a bunch of collages with my kids next to animals and their faces with stupid captions. I tag hundreds of accounts making sure celebrities are some. No one knows it's my account though.

What the fuck? People are reporting the page so it can be taken down. Fuck. I tell Alisa, Justin, and Josiah to come here.

"Angel from Montgomery said Charise does look like a fish," I lie. "She says Charise is the ugliest child I have."

I'm so pissed nobody's saying anything bad about my kids.

"Greg from Tampa says Justin and Josiah ain't shit," I lie. "They left their mom for dead."

I lie all night until my account is taken down.

Chapter 60

I can't stop staring at my kids. Charise started that bullshit ass conversation about me, which means she's the damn starting point of everything that's happened. Fuck this lil' girl. If she staying in my house, she gone definitely pay for what she did and said. I need to think of what I'm gone do to her.

I hear Josiah talking to Charise in the kitchen.

"I don't care what she asks you to do," Josiah says. "You just fucking do it."

Fuck it. I can get some water later. Josiah not gone get a day off. I know exactly how I'm gone do this.

When everyone's in a deep sleep, I wake Charise up and have her get in my bed. I get Josiah's ass and instruct him to take her virginity.

Charise fights him.

I'm drinking.

"Pull out Josiah," I say. "You can go to your room son."

"How do you feel Charise?" I ask. "Are you hurting? Your brother just raped you? How does it feel?"

"Can I go back to bed?" Charise asks.

"Why do you look like you're ready to walk out and tell the world what happened?" I ask. "You led your brother on. It was consensual."

"I'm not going to say anything," Charise says. "I just want to go to sleep."

"Get out," I say.

Chapter 61

I got an email from one of the ladies at the writer's photo-shoot. Her names Paula. She wants me to come back and do the interview again. She said something went wrong with the camera.

"So everyone's doing the interview again?" I ask.

I have her on the phone.

Paula gets quiet for a second and that silence tells me everything I need to know, but I want to see if she'll admit it or feed me some bullshit.

"Just a few people," Paula says.

Paula really about to play me for a fool. I felt some of them bitches and bastards staring at me wrong. They were staring at my eyebrows so damn hard with their bug eyes that they started to itch. Fuck this bitch on the phone thinking I'm stupid. I'm going to read her ass then hang up in her face.

"You sure you don't need me to do it again because people couldn't stop staring at my eyebrows?" I ask.

I hate that I have to say this shit.

"That's not it Leah," Paula says. "We just had issues with the camera."

"I know you're lying," I say. "I felt some of those heartless bitches staring at me. You should've hired a professional ass camera man who could've lied and said he needed to stop the interview for a second, instead of recording a bunch of dam footage he wouldn't be able to use. You don't think I know you're trying to protect those bitch's reputations? You don't want people to know they only look good on the outside, but their insides are black and muddy? I know they have this nice and clean-cut image they throw at the public and I came in the room and put that shit to the test. Man fuck doing that interview again and fuck each and every one of those heartless tramps. Just use my audio with a still of me."

179

I hang up.

Despite being angry behind people naturally looking at what's different disgustingly, I make a nice dinner. Greens, macaroni, potatoes, and baked chicken. Everyone enjoys it.

Once Bianca and Stacey finish, I dismiss them to their room. I have the rest of the clan line up outside the downstairs bathroom. I make them all shove their fingers down their throats and throw up dinner. Then I let them eat bologna and bread sandwiches.

The next day, I mix all types of nasty shit. Vegetable juice, milk, and eggs. I make my kids drink it after dinner and threaten to take a belt and whoop them if they throw it up.

Lanice can't keep it down.

I decide to hit them all because of her.

I have my oldest five come in my room at two in the morning.

They hop in my shower, get wet, and hop out. I hit them all then hear knocking on my bedroom door.

"Mommy we need to take punishment?" Stacey cries.

Her and Bianca are standing at the door prepared to pay for leaving the house against my will.

"No. I just caught your brothers and sisters trying to sneak out again so they're getting a whooping," I lie. "Go back to bed."

I pull a lighter out my drawer. I'm flicking it on and off to make them think I'm crazy. I'm smiling.

As I lie in bed, I'm thinking about Charise's I-want-to-act-ass impersonating me. I'm gone get her. I can't just let her get away with that shit. She's one of the main reasons everybody was laughing at me. She should've stayed her ass in bed. I can't think of what I want to do. I know I can't beat her too hard. She might die.

I call Charise in my room, make her hold her hands out and hit them over and over with the belt. I make Stacey and Bianca watch. After Charise's hands, I do her ass. She's lucky I let her keep her pants up. I call the rest of the crew to my room and give Charise center stage.

"Make me laugh," I say.

Charise is crying and can barely move.

"Do something!" I yell.

I'm one evil ass bitch right now. But I didn't deserve what happened to me. I didn't deserve none of that shit. These kids need to pay, not get a pass when time goes by. They need to understand how it feels. I can't live if they don't. I already got powerful people vouching for me not to put them in foster care. I already got to live with the bastards that fucked me still breathing.

I'm not letting these kids get away with shit.

They need to pay.

Chapter 63

I wake up in the middle of the night to use my bathroom. I hear Josiah and Justin in the living room.

"So start making the necessary friends and contacts because when I see those fucking bastards, I want they fucking necks," Josiah says. "I'm not gone let them get away with doing that to her. I'm just not."

"I say we hurt they asses now by fucking with they family," Justin says. "Houses, cars. Something to let them know that we gone come for them later. Something to make them lose sleep every night in they fucking cells."

"If we get caught we going to prison," Josiah says. "I'm only risking that if I get the mutha fuckas that did this shit to her."

"I want in," Charise says. "What's the plan?"

"We're working on it," Justin says.

I take my ass to bed. They not gone do shit.

The next few days, I repeat the same activities: make the kids have intercourse together, fight each other, vomit, get beat while they're wet, and stand in the cold.

They deserve everything they're getting, yet here I am crying.

I'm in my room sitting in the dark with a candle lit angry at myself because I can't get over what's happened to me.

I don't know why I can't stop crying. I'm getting even with the kids.

Why is my guilty conscience kicking in now?

I'm one abusing ass bitch. That's not who I used to be though.

My heads spinning trying to cope with everything I've done and justify it.

I call Mya.

"I need you to get me a few grams," I say.

"I got you," Mya says.

She brings me some marijuana.

"You want to smoke one with me?" I ask.

"Girl you ain't said nothing but a thang," Mya says. "Welcome to the club."

I ain't never smoked a day in my life. I drink a little, but never did too much because I always had my kids. I just started drinking more when I got abused.

"So what's up girl?" Mya asks lighting the blunt.

"Shit girl," I say. "Just trying to make it another day."

"How the kids?" Mya asks.

"Good and sorry," I say.

"They messed up bad, but I know they love you," Mya says. "The world's full of horny ass bastards that don't give a fuck about shit. I got three home-girls that were raped by their dad or brothers."

Bianca's running down the stairs.

"Momma Alisa hurt her arm," Bianca says.

I rush upstairs.

"What happened?" I ask.

"I just hit it on the wall," Alisa says. "I'm okay."

"You're okay?" I repeat giving her a hug. "You're crying. But whatever. You look beautiful."

I haven't said a kind word to any of my kids in a long time. I'm happy Alisa is hurt.

"Thank you," Alisa cries.

"For what?" I ask.

"The hug," Alisa says.

Mya is high as fuck.

"You gone be okay to drive home?" I ask.

"Girl yea," Mya says. "But on some real shit Leah, don't let this shit get the best of you. Don't let them dumbass men ruin your life or your relationship with your kids. You strong. I know you are. Keep them around. Watch them grow up. And most importantly, let them make you some money."

"Girl I know," I say. "Hell, my boys can make me a lot of money off dribbling that damn ball. I love them lil' knuckle

heads."

"You're blessed Leah," Mya says. "You're a good woman. You have a beautiful family. You got it girl. Shake that shit off. Believe it or not, it's people that's been through a lot worse than you."

"I think I'm gone start smoking with you more often," I say.

"What you trying to say?" Mya asks. "I'm better when I'm under the influence?"

"No. But you aren't scared to tap into that sentimental side when you are," I say. "I love you girl."

"You got some drank?" Mya asks.

I mix orange juice and liquor and let her know she's staying the night. We both sleep on the couch.

After all that drinking, I still can't sleep because I feel like I am this off, weird bitch, who won't stop thinking about everything my kids did to me.

My motive was to scar them like they did me. If they stayed home, I wouldn't have been raped. If they'd have never talked shit, I'd have never punished them.

I just got to accept that I needed to mistreat them to heal. Now their brain can deal with what mine is. They can understand what it's like to go through life with abuse traumatizing their brains. Most importantly, they can understand what I'm going through.

Chapter 64

"Mom Lanice needs a pad," Alisa says.

"First one to start huh?" I say, handing her the pad and a new pair of panties.

Alisa hasn't even gotten hers yet.

"I started early in the morning the day we snuck out to the game," Alisa says.

Wait. Was she going through a mood swing that day? Is the change in her body what caused her to go off like that?

I can't think about this right now. I can't make excuses for what any of the kids did. I've already said and done too much.

Chapter 65

Me and the kids board our private jet to Hawaii. It's very spacious. There's screens to watch movies on too.

The kids play cards and sleep the whole ride with a movie playing.

I just sleep.

A limo takes us to a beautiful mansion.

I give the kids permission to go in the house. There' s a lot of bedrooms. I could get used to this life. The fridge and cabinets are stocked with food and Ms. Eva gave me a few thousand to spend wherever I want.

I tour the backyard. There's a backhouse, basketball court and a pool and jacuzzi.

Alisa, Lanice, and Charise flat iron their hair.

The delivery man's here with the Chinese food, but I don't know the code for the gate. I ask the kids if they saw what our limo driver punched in and they say no.

Josiah spots a small sheet of paper on the fridge and finds the code. I kiss him on his forehead.

I feed my youngest two and put them in bed.

I put my red bikini on with my red pumps, pour me some wine, grab my purse and head to the backhouse where the kids are already sitting on the couch. And yes indeed. They all look nice in their two pieces and swim trunks.

"Alright you guys and lovely girls," I say. "I'm just gone flat out say it. I apologize for everything I've done. I messed up. I'm not trying to make excuses, but I really didn't know how to get over everything that's happened to me."

"Momma, you almost died," Charise says. "It's not your fault. We deserved it."

"I really wish I could've coped in a different way," I say.

"Let's just move forward Mom," Josiah says. "We've all messed up. You don't have to apologize to us. If it weren't for

our behavior, we wouldn't be having this conversation right now. We are the ones that are responsible for everything that's happened."

"To be honest Mom, I'm glad you did what you did to us," Justin says. "I wanted you to get back at us some kind of way. I wanted you to get even. We love you to death and we don't want anything to happen to you. You're our heart."

"I want you guys to forgive me," I say. "I'll never hurt you again."

"We forgive you Mom and we'll never disobey you again," Josiah says. "Now can you forgive us?"

I give my children hugs. I grab my purse and give them their phones back.

They're all so happy.

"They're back on," I say. "I promise I'll let you call everyone you haven't talked to in a while, but I want to show you guys something. It's important to me."

I pull a lighter out my purse.

"You see what abuse can do to a person?" I rhetorically ask.

I grab a sheet of paper and turn the lights off. I burn the paper and tell the kids that it represents me when I was being abused and some of my bones were broken.

"Blow it out," I tell Josiah. "That is what I was hoping would happen. I was hoping you would come and stop the burning. But you couldn't because you were so set on playing basketball."

"We'll make sure you never burn again Momma," Justin says. "We never want that paper to turn to ashes."

"So tonight is the night we start over," I say. "Let's enjoy our two weeks here and get back the love we once had."

We fill our bellies with shrimp fried rice, orange chicken and egg rolls, and wash it down with sodas.

These kids have put up with a lot of shit. However, I don't care about any sorry they say. Maybe it was just an off night. However, even if it was, it doesn't take away from the fact that

the whole world has access to that embarrassing shit. I'll never get past that. When I see people laugh at me, I'll have an instinct to think it's because of the video. My life will never be the same.

But like my son said: we need to move forward.

"Smile Mommy," Lanice says.

She takes a picture of me.

"Take a picture of me and Mommy together," Lanice tells Josiah.

Lanice runs her fingers through my hair and compliments me. Me and the kids take lots of pictures in the pool, in the jacuzzi and in the house. We also snap pictures of us eating.

We do a little late night swimming, then I have them join me in the jacuzzi for another intimate conversation.

"So this is what we're going to do," I say. "We're going to strategize things from now on. We're going to slowly but surely get people talking about us in a good way again. We gone do this and we gone do it right. We gone come so correct that everyone gone forget about the shit that's happened. We gone show people that we can't be broken. They know we're fresh from a troublesome time but we gone show them we can bounce back. We done show them that we aren't breakable."

The kids nod their heads. I can feel that they can't wait to show the world how big of a mistake they made bashing their mother. Most importantly, they can't wait to show everyone how they really feel about me.

They love me.

Yea. That's a lie.

Chapter 66

"Go ahead and make another *FriendSpot* and *ChitChatFam* account," I say to my kids.

I take a picture of all the kids in the jacuzzi.

Charise is crying. She forgot the password to one of her accounts that had negative pictures of me.

"Momma," Josiah says. "Is there any way we can get that video off the internet?"

"Once it's on the internet it's there forever son," I say. "Let it be a lesson to you."

Me and the kids race in the pool, swimming from one side to the other.

Then me and my oldest five go inside, line up, an dplay a scary game where we hold onto the person's waist in front of us. The person on the end has to drop off the line and hide while everyone else keeps walking, then jump out and scare us.

The lights are off and no one can talk. So the person that's second to last isn't supposed to let anyone know when the last person is gone.

The house is completely pitch black.

I'm the line leader.

I hear one of my boys scream.

"Who was that?" I ask.

I get no response.

I go in Lanice's room. When I walk past the closet, someone's beating on the door.

"Turn the light on," I say.

Bianca and Stacey are sitting on Alisa's bed.

"Where's Josiah?" Alisa asks.

"Right here," Josiah says walking out the closet. "I was coming to hide and Bianca and Stacey were up looking for us."

We all bust out laughing.

"Alright. Let's call it a night," I say.

Everyone goes to their rooms.

I cuddle with Alisa.

"I love you Mami," I whisper to her.

"I love you too," Alisa says.

Charise knocks on the door. She comes in and cuddles with us.

"I want to apologize for everything I've done to you girls," I say.

"It's okay Mommy. It's over," Charise says.

"I knew you could never get your virginity back," I say. "And I'm so very sorry. I really am. If you guys come up with something reasonable that you want, just let me know."

Alisa and Charise start crying. I've hurt them badly.

"Mommy it's fine," Alisa says. "We just want you to love us like you used to and things to go back to the way they were."

I kiss them both on their foreheads and we doze off.

Chapter 67

I ain't been doing nothing but stressing, eating, drinking and smoking.

Josiah and Justin are outside sitting on the bench writing by the basketball court.

"Come shoot with me?" I ask them.

They don't want to.

"You guys don't have to give this up because of what happened," I say.

They continue writing.

"You made a mistake," I say. "It's okay. I'm here. I know you love to play."

"Mom, they gone make us play with kids our age," Josiah says.

'Oh. Y'all too good for that?" I ask.

"I would want to play with the high school boys like I was doing before," Josiah says. "Otherwise I'd just rather not play."

"I feel like if we keep going, then people with think what you said is true," Justin says.

"I don't think you love sports more than me son," I say.

"If we play people will think that," Justin says.

"Don't worry about what people will think," I say.

"It's like every time I touch a ball now I think about what happened to you," Josiah says. "I picture everything you went through. I can't move forward with those memories. It's just best I don't play."

"I want everything to get back to the way it was and that includes everyone doing what they love," I say. "Now I want to tell you guys something, and let me say I'm not upset first. I know you're having sex. You're kids. You're going to make mistakes. I'm grown and I still make them. Hell, I had you guys young. The only reason I brought it up is because I want you to be safe. I don't want you guys catching any diseases."

I give them each two condoms.

"Be smart," I say. "A lot can be done with just a simple phone. And I'm referring to recordings and pictures. Don't do anything in public that you don't want to see or hear about the next day. When you get a little bit of fame, people get jealous. When you look good, people get jealous. They want to ruin you. Be smart and trust no one."

"Yes ma'am," Josiah says.

Me and the boys shoot around.

Chapter 68

My oldest crew have plenty of bags with them when me, Bianca and Stacey meet them at the food court at the mall.

"We kept getting stopped by people that wanted pictures and autographs," Lanice says.

"Justin, why you got that cake?" I ask.

"We'd rather eat cake than candy Mom," Justin says.

I get me, Bianca and Stacey some Chinese food. There's kids behind us that want pictures. There's also kids by my oldest five that want pictures. And because of them, my food isn't scalding hot like I like it when we sit down.

The kids and I hit up the beach and deal with the same thing. Kids keep wanting pictures and autographs.

"Mom, let's just stay home the rest of the trip," Lanice whispers to me.

To end the night off, I look up another house to move into when we get back to California.

I can't stay at the one I'm in now anymore. It's not comfortable and a pedophile knows where I live.

Alisa leads me to the backhouse.

I walk in and, "Surprise!" all my kids scream.

"Let us make it up to you Mom," Josiah says.

He walks me to the cake.

I was crippled during my birthday being that they snuck out the house and weren't able to defend me.

There's a disco ball and music playing.

"I would've bought you alcohol if I could Momma," Josiah says.

Everyone sings happy birthday to me. I forgot all my kids could sing. They sound professional.

"I appreciate this you guys," I say. "I love you so much."

"We love you too Mommy," Stacey says.

"We should've recorded it," I say.

"I did," Justin says.

"I got you coming in and blowing out your candles Mom," Alisa says.

Me and the kids dance and eat all night. I have everyone post a picture from my belated birthday party on their pages for the world to see.

I post one of all the kids around the cake.

I let Bianca and Stacey stay up late. I need to know what they want to focus on activity wise.

"So we got dancing, singing, acting, basketball again maybe," I say. "Tell me what's up so I can start figuring out how I'm gone balance everything between all seven of you."

"I want to do it all," Bianca says. "But not basketball."

Justin tickles her.

"Mom what do you want to do?" Alisa asks.

"We want you to be able to accomplish more of your dreams too," Josiah says. "We don't want your life to go on hold for us."

"I love you guys so much," I say. "Tell you what. All I need is my writing time. I don't mind devoting the rest of the time to you guys."

"I think we should all start with singing," Stacey says.

"It doesn't matter Mom," Josiah says. "Whatever you think is best is what we want to do."

"What I think is best is we try all those hobbies at once," I say. "All we need is good time management."

Chapter 69

The kids are writing songs and I'm writing scripts.

I buy three cameras and tripods for recording. I don't want to wait until we get back to California. We're going to record episodes of our web show here in Hawaii and write some songs.

Our show is centered on seven kids that get left home alone and spend their time doing all the things their mother doesn't let them: drive her cars around the house, wear her heels, watch R rated movies and binge on sweets. They're exciting time goes well until one of the characters, who will be played by Josiah, runs the car into a tree and the kids try to repair it themselves.

We teach ourselves how to work the cameras and our first three episodes are done within three days.

I edit and save them to my computer.

"How many songs do you have done?" I ask Josiah.

"I have three that I'm ready to record," Josiah says.

"What about everyone else?" I ask.

"I'm not sure," Josiah says.

He helps me hook my computer up to the TV. Me and the kids watch our shoe. My kids look so good on camera. All my kids are naturals when it comes to acting. They're really blessed.

Josiah kisses me on the cheek.

Chapter 70

"Momma, you ever wish you were one of those big stars on TV?" Charis asks me while we cuddle in bed.

"Now why would I want to be them?" I ask.

"Because on top of being happy, they have everything they want," Charise says.

"Let me tell you something Charise," I say. "Just because you see people smiling in front of those cameras does not mean they are happy. Money does not buy happiness. Happiness is priceless. The love we have as a family, you can't purchase anywhere."

"It's better to be poor and happy, than rich and sad, right Momma?" Charise asks.

"Right," I say.

"Can I tell you something Mom?" Charise asks.

"Anything," I say.

"I don't care what anyone says about you having us so young," Charise says. "I'm glad you're only a little older than us. We can grow old together."

"I still don't want you to go off and get pregnant young like I did," I say. "I didn't have any guidance growing up. My mother was never home or taught me a thing. But you guys have a loving mother. Y'all get under my skin sometimes, but I love each and every one of you to death. And I'm proud to be your mother."

We turn the movie on low and fall asleep.

Chapter 71

Me and Alisa play dress up and I put makeup on her face.

We're in the bathroom mirror adjusting her shirt so most of her stomach is showing. She tries on my heels and walks around the room in them.

"Take those off before you break your ankles," I say. "I do not feel like going to the hospital tonight."

"The hell," Alisa says.

"The hell what?" I ask.

"This shirt won't stay tucked under my bra," Alisa says. "Let's just get bikini ready and go to the pool. Grab us a drink Mommy."

I'm not bothered by her cursing.

Me and Alisa sit in the jacuzzi and sip wine. Alisa thinks she's grown. She puts on some music in the backhouse, cuts the disco ball on, and teaches me some seductive dance moves.

Afterwards, she cuddles close to me on the couch and we go to sleep.

Chapter 72

Me and Justin swim all night. He's having way too much fun throwing me up in the air and slamming me in this water.

I let him have a glass of wine as we walk around the front of the house. Then we sit on the front porch and listen to smooth Rhythm and Blues all night. He sings along and sounds just as good as the artist.

"You know you're really gifted right?" I ask.

"Thanks Mom," Justin says. "You're the one responsible for all these talented kids in the house. To me you gave us everything we have whether you taught it to us or not. You're our mother. Without us there's no you. I mean without you there's no us."

"I know what you meant son," I say. "It's all good."

We sleep on the couch together.

Chapter 73

Me and Josiah play basketball. He tackles me a few times to the ground just so he can kiss all over my face. He elbows me once and I fall pretending like I'm seriously injured. He picks me up and sees that I'm smiling.

I let him take a shot of alcohol and we make homemade nachos. We eat them outside on the bench.

"I want to be able to buy you all these things you want Mom," Josiah says.

"I know one day you'll be able to son," I say. "You're very gifted. I wish I was half as talented as you."

"You are Mom," Josiah says. "Just in a different way. You know how to write any and everything. You're successful. People come from all over to hear you speak. Mom, I admire you. Look at the life we have. You're able to hold it down with seven of us. We don't want for nothing."

"Son, I want to tell you something, and I'm telling you because you're the oldest," I say. "I heard y'all talking about getting revenge on the men that hurt me, and it's not worth it. I don't want to visit any of my kids in a juvenile facility or prison the rest of my life. We just gone have to trust that karma takes care of them."

"Well maybe it's up to us to give them karma," Josiah says.

"Son, listen to me," I say. "Just like you don't want to live without me, I don't want to live without you. I want you to promise me that you won't take it upon yourself to get revenge."

"I won't," Josiah says.

We play basketball and drink all night before we fall asleep in my room.

Chapter 74

It's our last day in Hawaii.

Me and the kids dress up real fancy and go to the backhouse. I have it decorated with glowing lights. The table has wine glasses and shot glasses on it with confetti surrounding them. I ordered Chinese and the music is playing low.

I hear Josiah say, "Mommy looks good."

We all take a shot of liquor. Stacey and Bianca take a shot of wine.

"The water is under the table," I say to the kids.

They all laugh.

We get our second shot and connect our glasses in the center of the table.

"This is to starting over and leaving the past behind us," I say.

"Cheers," we all say.

We eat, drink, and dance our last night.

Chapter 75

We're back in California.

I moved us into a new house. It has boxes all over the place, but I'm not going through any no time soon.

I invite Mya over despite the disorganization.

"Please tell me you brough some weed with you," I say.

"Of course," Mya says. "I like your new spot. How was Hawaii? Did y'all have a good time?"

"Yes girl," I say. "That's the most fun we ever had."

"That's good. I'm happy for you Leah," Mya says. "I mean it."

"Who you buy your weed from?" I ask.

"The shop," Mya says. "You should get a license. You got something to eat?"

I have Alisa make us a sandwich, chips and dip.

This damn blunt feels so good.

"You gone have to fight the boys off that one at school," Mya says.

"Believe me when I say it's not her I need to watch. It's them damn boys," I say. "the girls be thinking I'm they girlfriend and not they damn momma. They say all types of fucked up shit."

"That's crazy girl," Mya says.

"Yea girl," I say. "They call me ugly and worthless. Said I shouldn't leave the house. Just pick me a part from head to toe because they think I'm they competition."

"Girl if I ever have kids, I'm not gone even let them look at nobody that disrespects me," Mya says. "Let alone bring them in my house. Hell no."

Chapter 76

I wake up in the middle of the night to use the bathroom and peak in on the kids asleep. Josiah and Alisa aren't in their rooms. They're in the garage fucking against the wall like two grown ass people. They spot me and Josiah takes it upon himself to pump faster so he can finish before I walk up to them and pull them apart. I tell their naked asses to put some clothes on and get upstairs in my room.

I mix liquor and wine, take a big swallow, and make my way to my room.

I walk in and Josiah and Alisa's asses are kissing. I pull them apart.

What the fuck have I done? My kids are attracted to each other now.

"This needs to stop," I say. They're looking at me like it's my fault. And I know it is, but now it's up to me to stop this.

"We can't be like this," I continue.

"Go to you room Josiah," I say. "Alisa get your ass in my bed."

I roll a blunt and smoke it right in front of her. I don't give a damn right now. I've caused incest in my house. I got to think of something to get this out they system and without asking and damn body for help. Fuck. Josiah's ass didn't even wear a damn condom. This could get really bad.

I text the boys and tell them to meet me outside when everyone goes to sleep. I let them hit the blunt with me so they can relax and tell me everything I want to know at ease.

"She told me to meet her in the garage and that it was important," Josiah says. "Soon as I walked in, she shut the door and pulled my pants down."

"Did you resist?' I ask.

"No," Josiah says.

"Do you like fucking your sister?' I ask.

203

"Yes," Josiah says.

"What's it gone take for you to stop?" I ask. "When I said I wanted everything to go back to the way it was, that included not having no incest in my house. I want this shit to stop before I release any of our projects."

"You want me to stop Mom, I will," Josiah says.

I roll another blunt.

This shit is too much for me.

Chapter 77

Me and the kids spend the next month working on more episodes of our web show and recording songs.

I pay a beat maker.

I contact Coach Eric. I want the boys to give the team an apology.

We got to Coach Eric's house. I only have the boys and Alisa with me. We're the first ones to arrive.

"You guys want anything to drink?" Coach Eric asks.

"We're fine," I say.

Once everyone arrives, my boys stand in front of them.

"I want to start by saying I'm sorry for letting everyone down," Josiah says. "Coach did not have to give me the opportunity to play with such a great group of people that I look up to, but he did. He took a chance on me. And what did I do? I messed up at the worst time possible. At that time, I'm sure everyone knows what was going on with my mother. Me, my brothers and sisters made a mistake. We weren't supposed to play in the state championship. We disobeyed our mother and she almost died."

"I want to apologize as well," Justin says. "We let our emotions from our personal lives show on the court. We should've opened our mouths and told Coach how we were feeling so he could take us out. We hope that you guys can forgive us because we love this team. And if it's alright, we'd love to play with you guys again."

"I want to apologize to you Coach Eric for the fight that happened," I say.

"It's alright Ms. Rogers," Coach Eric says. "There's no hard feelings. I forgive you and I'm glad to see you recovered well. I'd love to have the boys come back and play another summer."

"We all would," one of the players say. "If it weren't for you two, we wouldn't have made it that far."

If my boys knew what was good for them, they'd pick another team. I bet all their teammates are gone whoop they asses real good when the time is right. They gone hurt them so bad they won't even be able to play.

I care none.

The doorbell rings. Coach Eric is looking like who the hell is at his door.

"I ordered pizza, wings and salad for everyone," I say.

At least I thought it was the pizza man.

"Justin go talk to Grace! Graces's sister yells.

What the hell is really going on? Grace's sister just walks in the house.

"Stop yelling at my damn son!" I scream.

I grab Justin and we go outside.

"Why the fuck would you invite her here?" I ask Justin. "And what the fuck is your problem?" I ask Grace's sister.

Before I can get an answer, Alisa starts punching the hell out of Grace in the driveway. I break the fight up.

This shit is blowing me. We're in Coach Eric's driveway and I have no idea what the fuck is going on.

"Did I do something to you?" Grace asks Justin crying.

Alisa slaps Grace.

"Don't do it again damnit!" I yell.

"Why do you think you did something to him?" I ask Grace.

"He's been ignoring me," Grace says.

"You don't disrespect our mother and expect us to still fuck with you," Alisa says.

"Take your ass in the house," I say to Alisa.

"We heard what you said about our mom," Justin says. "She's ugly huh?"

"Justin that was a long time ago," Grace says. "And I didn't mean it."

"Well you should've told us a long time ago, then we wouldn't be standing here right now because I would've never

liked you," Justin says.

I'm left outside with Grace and her sister who I want to choke so damn bad.

"Look, I'll talk to him tonight okay," I say to Grace's sister. "But right now is not the time. I don't appreciate you guys having no respect for this man's house. How did you know we were here?"

Grace's sister ignores me and goes to her car.

"Come on Grace," her sister says.

They pull off and the pizza man pulls up.

While the kids eat, I apologize to Coach Eric again.

Justin, Josiah and Alisa say they didn't tell the girls we would be here. So does everyone else in the house, but someone here did. Now that whoever the stupid snitch is sees the outcome, of course he's not gone say he gave the location.

Despite what just happened, the boys still have a good time.

They're outside eating pizza.

I chill inside with Coach Eric. He wants me to put the boys in public school so they can keep playing. The kids pursuing acting and singing prevents that. They need to have an open schedule.

Coach Eric tries over and over to come up with a way for them to pursue their careers and still go to public school.

I keep telling him no.

Chapter 78

"Ms. Eva wants us to come on her show again," I tell the kids. "Do you guys want to do it?"

They all say no.

"Good, because I don't either," I say. "Let our work ethic make the noise."

We post Episode One of *Kids Got the Nerve* and Josiah and Justin's *I Love My Mama.*

"Mom, let's celebrate tonight," Alisa says and winks at me.

I make us a home cooked dinner and wine to drink.

Me and the girls have on booty shorts and tank tops. The boys pay us no mind.

I release and episode of one of our shows every week.

I get calls and emails for the kids to perform, go on talk shows and make appearances. We do everything except the talk shows. The hosts aren't slick. Even though they're offering to let the kids perform, they still are going to require them to answer a few questions. We don't want to answer any. We know some questions will be negative.

A magazine company offers to pay for my oldest five to do some print modeling.

We go.

The company absolutely loves it when my kids get on set. These kids are just too damn good at everything they do. Their facials and poses are on point.

Bianca and Stacey get requested to do a few toy commercials. Alisa walks the runway in a few modeling shows. All the kids guest star on a few TV shows.

Our lives are busy.

And I don't mind. Our bills are getting paid.

With the kid's money.

Chapter 79

I'm sitting in my room watching Celebrity Info: On the Spot.

The reporters don't say a single bad word about my family. They just praise our talents. This is what we wanted all along. I cut the TV off when the lady stops talking about us. I only watch the gossip shows and read blogs to see what people are saying about me and my kids.

I can't really construct a book right now. The only topic I have is the abuse that the world already knows.

I take Charise with me to the store. After picking out a few oranges, I turn around and she's helping a little girl that's autistic who fell on the floor.

Charise gives her a hug. Then she opens the door for a lady in a wheelchair.

"Mommy is so proud of you baby," I say to Charise. "I think I want to let you guys have a Halloween party now."

We pick out some food for the party.

Charise texts her friends on the way home.

Chapter 80

I have orange and white lights hanging inside and outside of my house. Food and drinks are on the table. I have plastic silverware, plates and cups. I have a disco ball going and music playing.

While my kids put on their costumes, I order pizza and wings.

"Let me get a picture of everyone in their costumes before people start coming," I say.

The kids stand against the wall and I snap a group photo.

Stacey is a pumpkin. Bianca is a crayon. Lanice is a princess. Charise is an angel. Alisa is a belly dancer. Justin is a warrior and Josiah is a king.

The party is a success. The basketball team comes. Alisa's dance team shows up. Mya brings some of her cousins to play with Bianca and Stacey. Lanice and Charise invited some of their new celebrity friends.

Me and Mya sip wine by the den door where Bianca, Stacey and their new friends are playing.

"I want to take them around to a few houses," I say.

"Go ahead," My says. "I'll stay here."

"You sure you gone be able to handle all these grown ass kids?" I ask.

"Yea. They not too old to get they ass beat," Mya says.

I take Bianca and Stacey around to a few houses to get candy with their new friends. Feels good to get some fresh air. I wish I didn't have to hear these damn chainsaws though. That shit is scaring me.

The house is still in one piece when I get back.

When everyone leaves, there's only a few cups and napkins on the floor. At least nothing spilled on my carpet.

Me and the kids clean up the next day.

Chapter 81

"Can we have another party?" Stacey asks.

They not having another party like that for a minute. One is enough for at least a year for me. I don't like having all those kids in my house.

We chill in the den. Charise is on her computer looking shocked.

"What?" I ask.

"Look," Charise says.

Their videos have over a hundred million views and we've now racked up enough money to rent out the Star Lanes Center, where professional sports games take place.

I call the arena and get the confirmation that we can put on our own show there.

"You guys are putting on a concert at Star Lanes next month," I say.

The kids are hugging each other and screaming happily.

"Alright. Everybody sit back down so I can map everything out," I say.

Bianca is hugging me and crying.

"Thank you Mommy," Bianca says.

"Okay, so I'll do the lighting, fog machines, and wind machines," I say. "I'll reserve studios for practice. I'll also set up a meeting with the DJ."

"Mom make sure you add in some extra instrumentals so we can dance," Josiah says.

"I got you son," I say.

We spend weeks in the studio working on choreography.

Sometimes the kids have a hard time falling asleep every night because they can't wait to perform at Star Lanes.

Chapter 82

It's showtime.

Me and the kids are at Star Lanes Center.

It's sold out.

The kids sing the songs they wrote and dance to them. There's a lot of big screens projecting them bigger so the people in the back can see them.

There's people that hold their hands out to be touched by my kids, but there's no way my kids can touch all of them. There's people crying too.

There's equipment that lifts the kids higher and there's wind machines.

The kids love being celebrities.

We stay up late watching footage from their concert.

I check my email and have another one from Ms. Eva. I tell the kids we're going to do her show again. They're not hype at all, but I feel like we owe her. She didn't have to give us a paid vacation.

The next week I get invited to the Frankie Show to talk about my books. The crowd gives me a huge round of applause as I walk on stage.

There's a little girl and her mom sitting next to Frankie.

"So how have you been Ms. Leah?" Frankie asks.

"I'm good," I say. "And yourself?"

"Really good," Frankie says. "Thanks for asking. Let me start by saying congratulations on all your success. You're very talented and your books have inspired so many people."

We talk about my book *Behind the Cover* and how I came up with the story line. Frankie says it's her favorite book. She says lots of celebrities gave me good critiques. She even gives the audience a copy of my book and a book mark.

"I produce the show *Single Not Gone Work*." Frankie says. "I wanted to ask you to appear on a few episodes."

"I would love to come on your show Frankie," I say.

Frankie gives me a ten thousand dollar check.

"Now I know it's only a little, but I want you to start saving up and bring those characters to the big screen," Frankie says.

"I need help," the little girl sitting next to Frankie whines. "Please help me Leah."

"Let's go to a commercial break and real quick," Frankie says. "Leah, I was going to ask you backstage to give her a few words."

"About what?" I ask.

"Tell me what helped you please," the girl whines.

"Helped me what? What are you assuming I needed help with?" I ask. "What is she talking about Frankie? What did you tell her I needed help with?"

"I had someone call and ask you if you were okay with this," Frankie says.

"Okay with what?" I ask. "All I was told was we're discussing my profession. Nothing else. I wasn't told anything about any special guests."

"So let me apologize. I thought one of my staff members prepped you on Unique and her mom Cassie coming today," Frankie says. "Now I want to ask you before the cameras come on if you can give her a few words of wisdom on how you deal with people staring at you in ways you don't like."

"My sister killed herself because she couldn't deal with people staring at her nose mean," Unique says. "Your eyebrows Leah. How do you deal with them? I don't want to end up like my sister."

"This definitely should've been ran by me ahead of time," I bitterly say.

The camera man points to Frankie. The shows back on the air.

"Can you give her some advice?" Frankie asks.

"I don't have any," I say.

"Look Leah," Cassie says. "I know this isn't easy for you, and

I'm sorry no one told you about our visit. If you could say anything to her, give her any advice, I would be forever thankful. I'd really appreciate it."

Truth be told, no one said anything to me growing up to help me. How the hell is talking about what makes me different going to make me feel like I'm just like everyone else.

My own relative was the first person to make me start looking at my eyebrows more often in the mirror. Her sorry ass doesn't even know. Cassie needs to homeschool her daughter if she's having that many issues at school. I would. If she sees the girl still can't handle it and is going off on the deep end like her sister that jumped out the window, then I suggest she get her daughter surgery.

"I don't have any advice," I say.

I head backstage. Unique wraps her arms around me tightly crying. I'm frustrated as hell.

"Can you please get your daughter off of me?" I bitterly ask.

Cassie doesn't move. Frankie has to get Unique off of me so I can go backstage for a minute and get away from this bullshit ass conversation.

All I'm thinking about is Frankie's trifling ass and Unique. She wants to know what helps me. What helps me is not going around any and every one that will constantly remind me of my bushy eyebrows. If insecure people need a mentor, it's not me. Who the hell would want to sit around all day and talk about what makes them get talked about negatively?

I will be honest and say Unique is not the best looking child. I just don't like how she looks. Her face is not pretty to me. And that's what everyone sees first.

I have a gift I brought for Frankie. She's still on stage talking to Cassie. I was hoping Cassie was gone already. This means Unique is somewhere floating around because she is definitely not on the stage right now.

"Here Frankie," I say. "I was supposed to bring this when I

214

first came out, but I guess I forgot."

It's a pair of gold earrings.

On my way backstage I catch a little girl staring at Unique's face in a weird way. My body naturally slows down walking.

Unique hasn't noticed the girl looking at her yet.

I watch Unique walk on stage. The girl staring at her follows behind her.

Damn. Unique turned to the girl.

"Stop!" Unique cries.

The little girl makes a worse face.

It's still packed in the audience too. No one has left.

"Stop!" Unique yells again.

Unique pushes the girl and she falls straight to the floor. Unique feels bad and tries to help the girl up, but the girl runs to her dad, who is one of the crew members, and Unique runs backstage.

Cassie runs after her daughter.

"No!" someone screams.

This can't be fucking serious. Unique was almost successful in jumping off the second floor. Her mom caught her just in time.

I take a seat in front of Frankie. Cassie hold Unique and sits next to Frankie.

"Unique you are beautiful," I say. "There's nothing wrong with you."

Frankie thinks I didn't see her motion for one of the camera men to start recording.

"Everybody has something about them they wish was different," I say. "Eyes, nose, mouth, hair length. Boobs. But none of that matters. You're here and there's a lot of people that care about you and want you to stay. You're thinking about all the people that look at you wrong, but what about the ones that smile at you? The ones that play with you? The ones that invite you to their birthday parties? Don't you want to see them again?"

"Unique she asked you a question," Cassie says.

215

Unique still doesn't say anything.

"Well, think about those people. They're the ones that matter," I say. "That's what I did."

I'm tired of lying to her, but I have to say what this suicidal kid needs to hear. Truth is, I never get over people looking at me weird. I never forget who these people are. I have their faces stored in my memory. I can remember where I was at and what I was doing when they looked at me in a way I didn't want them to. My mind just stretches too far back.

I'm definitely too smart to believe that everybody has something about them they don't like.

I'm not for babying this fucking girl either.

"How did you make it to twenty-seven without taking the wrong way out like my other daughter?" Cassie asks.

I want to say I stayed away from annoying ass people like the ones in my face now, but that wouldn't be good for television.

"I focused on the positive people," I say. "My friends. My kids. I stayed busy."

Sometimes I would even stare at people the same way they stared at me. It felt good sometimes.

"I want to thank you so much Leah," Cassie says.

"Leah I'm very proud of you and your kids," Frankie says. "How are the kids?"

"I don't want to talk about anything else," I say. "I just want to go home."

I don't like to be broke down so I can build someone else up.

Chapter 83

Me, Mya and Marissa go to the bar. As soon as we sit down we both realize this was a bad mistake. Vayda and one of her buddies area at the table behind us. I'm facing them, Mya's back is to them. I already know they're about to start talking slick.

"Girl, I'm not in the mood," I say. "Let's just go."

"Hell no," Mya says. "They not running me away from my gourmet burger."

The waiter takes our orders and now Vayda has the confirmation she needs that we will be here for a while.

"Yea that's right," Vayda says to her buddy. "Lil' Charise wants me to be her mom. Guess she got tired of you and your bushy eyebrows raising her. I wonder what it was like being gang banged. Those men must've been pretty desperate to lay with that."

"Girl don't worry about that shit," Mya says.

"Last time I checked I still have all seven of my kids," I say. "And me and my baby daddy didn't have to take parenting classes. Yea my little Charise posted that video of you. She posted it because I made her."

Anyways. Me and my crew enjoy our food. I don't talk about the interview because I know Vayda and her buddy can hear.

"Let's go back to your place after this," I say to Mya.

When we get ready to leave, Vayda's buddy punches me in the back of my head. Mya pushes her before she can punch me again. I punch Vayda's buddy in her face. Then I punch Vayda in hers.

This bitch Vayda wants to pretend like she's so fucking hood but can't fight. She keeps pushing me and pulling my hair. Her punch is weak as fuck.

The security finally gets alerted of our fight and they break it up.

Chapter 84

My follows behind the two police cars that have me and Vayda in one and Vayda's buddy in the other one.

A man in a nice suit approaches us when we walk in the jail. The cops tell him what happened at the bar.

"Write them a ticket and let them go," the man in the nice suit says. "We don't have the space. I don't want to hear it. Let them go."

I couldn't be happier these handcuffs are off. I hop in the car with Mya and we go to the liquor store.

I'm so fucking angry. I can't believe that bitch really wanted to fight me. I want to fuck that bitch up so bad.

"Don't even trip off tonight," Mya says.

"Today was just not my fucking day," I say. "Frankie set me up to talk to that Unique girl, without telling me ahead of time what she was using me for."

"That's fucked up," Mya says. "Did you end up telling her anything?"

"I told her something after she tried to jump off the second floor," I say.

We both take a shot in the car.

"I wish I had a bottle to throw at Vayda's head," I say.

"That would've been nice," Mya says.

"The only reason she's relevant is because of her face," I say. "All she has to do is offer people head and she'll get what she wants."

"You jealous?" Mya asks.

"Girl hell no I ain't jealous," I say. "Why the fuck would I be jealous of a bitch that doesn't know the only reason she's getting ahead is because of what she looks like?"

"You think that shit hit the blogs yet?" Mya asks.

"Hell yea," I say. "Thanks for having my back."

"You know I got you," Mya says.

I have a hangover when I get home.
"Mom are you okay?" Josiah asks.
He's seen the news.
"I'm fine," I say.

Chapter 85

"Don't' beat yourself up Charise. It's okay," I lie.

Everything Vayda said, she must've read on a blog, or maybe heard on the damn news.

"Let me take a nap," I say.

I can't fall asleep because I'm thinking about everything Vayda said.

On top of that, I hear Charise laughing. My life is fucked and it all started because her little ass went on a rant. She doesn't deserve to be happy.

"Mommy you want to play charades with us?" Lanice asks.

Now I'm thinking about Bianca's acting ass getting upset because of my eyebrows.

"No Sweety. Thanks though," I say.

They earned all that shit I did to them. They fucked up my mind. Whenever I do through a mental breakdown, they are my release. I don't deserve to be uncomfortable and unhappy while they sit in their rooms and play games like nothing ever happened.

"Don't let Vayda get under your skin," Josiah says. "She ain't shit."

"Watch your mouth son," I say.

"For real Mom," Josiah says. "Don't let that child abusing bitch make you lose any sleep."

"I'm gone pop you on your mouth the next time you curse boy," I say.

Chapter 86

Me and Charise are staying home while Evan takes my kids to the movie theater.

I push Charise to the ground.

"What did I do?" Charise cries.

"What do you think you did?" I ask. "You didn't think my mind would be washed clear did you?"

I'm laughing watching her cry.

"Every day for the rest of my life I have to worry about someone chastising me about the shit you said," I say. "Not only am I a rape victim, but I have a daughter who admitted to the world she thinks I'm ugly. I have a daughter that put thoughts in my mind that I don't want. I have a daughter that has said things about me my worst enemy has never said to me. I have a daughter that I will never know if she truly ever loved me."

"Mommy I am sorry about everything and I do love you," Charise cries. "I'm not acting."

"How do I know that you're not lying?" I ask.

"Because I've been well-behaved," Charise says. "I've been helping you whenever you want and letting you know how much I love you."

I push her to the ground and grab a rope. I tie her arms behind a chair and tie her legs together. Her mouth is taped shut.

"I don't want to hear anymore lies," I say.

I grab a liquor bottle and sit in front of my daughter.

"You know me being raped and all that was because of everyone," I say. "But the video. That fucking video you decided to release has made me a lot of enemies. Vayda is one person, but there's a lot of damn people that ride for that bitch."

I slap Charise and pull the tape off her mouth a little.

"What did you say?" I joke.

"I thought we were past this," Charise says. "I thought you forgave us?"

I cover her lips back.

"I do forgive you guys," I say. "But pain is temporary, and my thoughts are permanent. And I'm tired of memories I don't want floating in my mind. So it's only right that you get pain when I want. You should have to live with bad memories too. Right?"

I punch Charise on her back. Then I hit her with a belt.

"From now on, I don't want to see you smile or laugh because I'll know exactly where your laughter is coming from," I say.

I remove the tape halfway off her mouth.

"What do you want to say?" I ask.

"Mommy can we rehearse this scene another time?" Charise asks. "My stomach hurts."

She winks at me.

"I think we have enough footage for our website and the blogs," Charise says. "I'm cramping and need to use the bathroom."

I'm looking out my peripheral vision trying to see what she sees.

Fuck.

My camera on the tripod is recording. It's hooked up to a live stream on the computer. The kids were using it earlier.

"It's okay. Untie me," Charise says. "We can finish up later."

Police sirens are nearing the house. I'm going to jail.

"Listen," Charise says. "We were filming. That's it."

"I'm going to jail," I say.

"Oh Mommy," Charise says.

Cops are beating on the door. I open it and the policewoman puts me in handcuffs.

"We were filming!" I yell. "What's this about!?"

"Where's the rest of the kids?' the policewoman asks.

"What is this about?" I yell again getting in the back of the police car.

"What did she do?' Charise yells. "Mommy!"

Chapter 87

I take my mugshot and then get taken to a cell.

In my cell, one butch looking lady is staring at my vagina area and smoking. Another lady keeps crying that she doesn't have long to live. Two other women are playing a game with their knuckles. They're trying to make each other bleed.

Now I'm stuck in a cell with the memories of my abuse.

Now my future is ruined.

"How long you doing?" the lady smoking asks me.

"I don't know," I say.

"You know jails not as bad as everyone makes it out to be," the lady smoking says.

"Oh really," I say. "You like being confined in a small cell?"

"It's not so bad," the lady smoking says. "You get used to it after a while. My advice is don't be antisocial. That's when all those suicidal thoughts come."

Chapter 88

Mildred and Tiffany bail me out of jail. I get in the van with them and my girls. My boys are in the car with Mya.

The kids eat pizza while me, Mildred and Tiffany sit in my den.

Mildred closes the den door and slaps me.

"What's gotten into you?" Mildred asks.

"If I'd have known the public would react like that, I would've never wrote the script," I say.

Mildred slaps me again.

Alisa comes in and asks, "Mom are you okay?"

"Yea, I'm fine," I say. "Close the door."

"Leah do you think we're fucking stupid?" Mildred asks. "Look."

Mildred shows me scars on her back.

"My mother did this to me mad at the bastards that raped her," Mildred says. "For years I wanted to turn her in, but I knew what she was dealing with. I knew she couldn't handle what happened to her. I never gave up on her. She gave up on herself and overdosed on cocaine. She left me and my three brothers here along knowing our dad didn't want us."

"Leah you are very fortunate," Tiffany says. "The woman that came to get Charise was my sister. If she didn't know we knew each other, she'd be on her way to a foster care center."

"I asked the kids if they wanted to remain with you and they all said yes," Mildred says. "I told them what to say so they didn't end up getting adopted by some gold-digging parents or a pedophile. You do know that's what can happen to any of the kids in the system right?"

"Your kids did a good job lying for you," Tiffany says.

"Now we helped you and all we want in return is for you to take one parenting class," Tiffany says. "And to promise us you will never lay another hand on your kids."

"Can we have your word?" Mildred asks.

"Yes," I say.

"Don't mess up the blessing you have," Mildred says. "You have a beautiful family. Don't ruin it."

Chapter 89

Charise lays in the bed with me.

"Why'd you lie for me?" I ask.

"Because I love you," Charise says. "I can't live without you Mom. I know I said mean things, but I didn't mean them. I never want to be without you, and I never want to hurt your feelings."

"I want to thank you for looking out for me even while I was down there hitting you," I say.

"You're welcome," Charise says. "Please don't question whether I'm sorry or not again."

"I won't baby," I say.

I hear Lanice screaming.

Earlier this morning I took one of Charise's hair clamps and replaced the metal party with scissor blades. Lanice used it and now most of her hair is on the floor.

"Lanice baby, why'd you cut your hair?" I ask.

"We need to write a complaint to the store," Bianca says.

Josiah and Justin walk in, see the hair on the floor and walk out.

"Don't worry about it," I say. "You're beautiful with or without long hair. If you want, we can get you a sew-in."

Chapter 90

I attend the parenting meeting I promised Tiffany and Mildred.

Mya's watching the kids.

I'm not listening to the lectures or the videos in class. I don't need to be taught how to raise my kids. There's nothing anyone can tell me about the kids that came out of my stomach.

I buy me and the kids some chili cheese fries on the way home.

"Oh my goodness these are so good," Stacey says.

I ask the boys if they want to watch a scary movie with me. Justin changes what he's looking at on his phone.

They both say yes.

"Do you miss Grace?" I ask Justin. "Son it's okay for you to give her a second chance. Look at everything we've all said and done. I know you like her. I say give it a second try. If you still feel like you don't want nothing to do with her, then let her go."

"No Mom. I'd feel like a food," Justin says. "Only an idiot would go back to a girl that disrespects his mother. I couldn't live with myself knowing that every time I bring her around, you have to deal with bad memories. The next time anyone says anything bad about you, please just tell me. I don't want to find out from somebody else."

"I love you son," I say.

"I love you too," Justin says.

Me and the kids watch movies until we fall asleep.

Chapter 91

Mildred and Tiffany call and ask how the parenting class went.

"I needed it," I lie.

Me and the kids go to Mya's so they can get in the pool.

Josiah bumps into a lady and she is pissed.

"Watch where you're fucking going!" the lady shouts. "Stay out the way you no good kid!"

"Sorry," Josiah says.

The lady's towel falls and Josiah goes to pick it up. She pushes him.

"Don't' touch my shit," the lady bitterly says and walks out the gate.

The kids all looked at me while the lady fussed at Josiah, but I knew I wasn't helping him. Now they know what it feels like when the people they thought would always have their back don't.

Chapter 92

Alisa started her period again, and this time she wants my help.

I run her some bath water.

"You okay?" I laugh.

"Stop Mommy," Alisa says.

"It's a part of life," I say. "Don't be upset."

Alisa asks me to make her some soup.

"You started your period. You didn't get sick," I say.

I almost touch the stove while it's hot. Alisa moves my hand.

I hope this isn't the first sign of mental illness.

Me and my kids continue to live together.

We still have a lot of issues but we manage.

www.ingramcontent.com/pod-product-compliance
Lightning Source LLC
Chambersburg PA
CBHW031108260626
47172CB00001B/268